# Sudden Death

Lew Harper receives news that his father is having trouble and spares no time getting back there to help him out. But Lew is too late and the Circle H ranch is in the grip of a stranger.

Looking for explanations, Harper finds himself in an unexpected ambush and his troubles escalate wildly, taking a strange turn when he discovers that his father has actually been missing for three years. Every way he turns the mystery deepens and, when the shooting starts, sudden death is on the cards, and it won't stop until Lew has all the answers. . . .

# Sudden Death

Corba Sunman

A Black Horse Western

ROBERT HALE · LONDON

© Corba Sunman 2012
First published in Great Britain 2012

ISBN 978-0-7090-9759-4

Robert Hale Limited
Clerkenwell House
Clerkenwell Green
London EC1R 0HT

www.halebooks.com

Typeset by
Derek Doyle & Associates, Shaw Heath
Printed and bound in Great Britain by
CPI Antony Rowe, Chippenham and Eastbourne

# ONE

Lew Harper rode with a sense of urgency that had gripped him from the moment he received the letter from his father. In the five years since he had left home at eighteen to escape the humdrum life of a cowpuncher, he had come to realize that he had made a bad mistake in turning his back on the Circle H ranch in Kansas, which he had called home during his formative years. Pride, and the determination to succeed in life, had prevented him from returning to his father, Frank, and admitting that he had been wrong. But the letter changed all that. It contained a cry for help, and Lew dropped everything, boarded a train in Montana, and rode it to Buffalo Crossing, which was the point nearest to the Circle H. There he had bought a horse and set out to ride the forty miles to Dead Horse Creek and home range.

He rode steadily, his blue eyes noting half-forgotten landmarks while his mind puzzled over the contents of his father's letter, for Frank Harper was a product of the times and the location of his life and would not ask for help, not even from his eldest son, unless it was a matter of life and death. But no matter how Lew looked at the situation, or how many times he read the letter, he could find nothing between the scrawled lines that hinted at the trouble enveloping Circle H.

Tall and broad-shouldered, at twenty-three he was a handsome man that attracted a second glance from every woman he encountered. His light-coloured hair curled at the nape of his neck. His features were regular, although there was a serious cast to his tight-lipped mouth and a hint of shadow in his blue eyes, as if his experiences away from home had not all been pleasant. He wore dark-coloured range clothes of good quality and a yellow neckerchief, easing the air of grim determination that formed an aura about him. His red shirt carried the shape of a law star on its left breast pocket which, having been worn for three years, had prevented the sun from fading the material under it. He had a cartridge belt around his lean waist, with a tied down holster on his right hip containing a Colt .45 Peacemaker. Complementing his personal armament, a .44.40 Winchester rifle nestled in the saddle-boot on the right side of his black horse, its polished butt ready to hand just inside his right thigh.

When he topped a rise and saw Dead Horse Creek shimmering in the afternoon sunshine he reined in and tried to relax, for now he was on home range, and the headquarters of the Circle H ranch was situated just beyond the next ridge. His eyes narrowed as he looked around at familiar pastures that he had thought never to see again. But the old restlessness was gone now from his mind, driven out by the last three years of tough living as a deputy sheriff, into which he had drifted to avoid the hopeless grind of a cowhand's occupation.

A faint movement to the left caught his attention and he frowned and traced it to a saddle horse that had surmounted the rise ahead and was galloping down the slope along a trail which he knew led to a neighbouring ranch. He tensed, for the rider was raising dust as if pursued by the Devil himself. He screwed up his eyes in an attempt to recognize the figure in the saddle but the distance was too great, and he shrugged. It was none of his business if someone was trying to kill a good horse.

Then a second figure appeared over the rise, also travelling fast, but the rider reined in, jerked a rifle from its saddle-boot and raised it to his shoulder. A moment later, Lew saw a puff of gunsmoke, followed shortly by the crack of a shot, which echoed and re-echoed across the vast emptiness of the range. Lew straightened in his saddle and touched spurs to his horse. Someone was in trouble, and as this was Circle H range it could be his father on the receiving end of the shooting.

The leading rider was raising dust along the trail, and soon vanished into a stand of timber to Lew's left. Moments later a rifle cut loose from the cover of the trees and the pursuing rider turned his horse abruptly and rode into a convenient draw that took him out of sight. Lew reined in and sat his horse on a tight rein, listening to the fading echoes of the shooting until they died away. He looked left and right for signs of either rider, but the man on the leading horse did not reappear, and there was no more shooting from him. The second rider emerged from the draw and rode back towards the crest where he had initially appeared. Lew frowned as he turned in the same direction, for Circle H lay just beyond the ridge.

He stayed out of sight of the rider, and kept off the crest when he reached it, dismounting just off the skyline and trailing his reins. He crawled to the crest and peered at the small ranch headquarters down by a meandering stream. A sigh escaped him as he took in the familiar sight, and he was reminded how, in Montana, he had wished he had never left home. He watched the rider that had chased the man on the white horse dismount beside the corral, and Lew let his gaze roam over the rest of the spread.

Everything looked exactly the same as he remembered, except that his father's old rocking chair was no longer on the porch; for a moment he had a startlingly clear image of the old man seated on that chair after a long day's work. His gaze shifted to a knoll beyond the house and he saw the stark outline of a stone cross mounted on a rock, marking his mother's grave. He could not remember his mother for she had died of a fever when he had been barely five years old.

The man below took care of his horse and then went to the house, which he entered as if he owned the place. Lew exhaled deeply and went back to his own horse. He mounted, ascended the rise and rode down the slope towards the ranch. There were questions in his mind which he hoped the unknown man below could answer.

He was halfway across the hard pan of the yard when the man emerged from the house and halted on the porch, cradling a Winchester in his arms. He was tall and over-large, with a blocky figure, wide shoulders, and thick, muscular arms. His face was moon-shaped, features fleshy, except for his lips, which were thin and drawn tightly

8

against his teeth. He looked like a man of mean disposition, and his habitually narrowed eyes carried an ill-humoured expression. He was wearing range clothes but did not look like a cowpuncher. He watched Lew's approach, his thick legs apart; his ungainly body teetered unsteadily on the balls of his feet. He remained motionless until Lew reined up in front of the porch.

'Who in hell are you and what do you want?' demanded the man hoarsely, his voice sounding as if it came up from his boots. His tone was belligerent, containing impatience and a trace of barely concealed insolence.

Lew regarded him for several moments, not liking his manner.

'You sound like your name could be John Pig,' Lew observed at length.

'Do you reckon you could teach me some manners? If you're on the prod then get off that horse and see how far you can get.'

Lew ignored the invitation. He held his reins in his left hand; his right hand lying on his thigh just forward of the butt of his holstered pistol. He watched the rifle in the stranger's hands, and was geared for quick action should the muzzle of the long gun lift towards him.

'I asked you a question,' the man snarled. 'Who are you and what are you doin' on private property?'

'That's what I'm wondering about you,' Lew said quietly. 'How come you're standing on that porch as if you own the place?'

'I work here, and I'm doing the job I get paid for, which is to keep drifters and no-goods from moving in. So what's your reason for coming here?'

9

'I was on the rise back there when you fired a shot at a rider on a white horse heading along the trail to the Box W ranch. Who were you shooting at?'

'That ain't none of your business. Now get out of here before I start shooting at you.'

'Try that and you'll make the biggest mistake of your life. I'm Lew Harper. My father owns this spread. So where is he?'

The man's face did not change expression but his eyes flickered, and the muzzle of his Winchester, which had been pointing at the sun-warped boards of the porch, lifted a fraction. Lew's right hand moved at the same instant, and his pistol appeared in his hand in a blur of speed. He pointed the muzzle at the man, and the three clicks that sounded as he cocked the weapon filled the air with sudden menace.

'Just open your hands and drop the rifle,' Lew said patiently.

The man blinked at Lew's fast draw, and didn't need a second telling. His fingers loosened their grip and the Winchester clattered on the boards at his feet. He let his hands drop to their full length and stood unmoving, his dark eyes fixed in an unblinking stare at Lew.

'You're a gunhand,' he said shortly, his lips barely moving. 'You've been sent in here to cause trouble, huh? I've been told to watch out for troublemakers. That feller I chased off a while ago looked like he wanted to cause trouble.'

'What's your handle?' Lew demanded harshly.

'I'm Cleaver Nolan.'

'Where's my father?'

'Frank Harper.' Nolan spoke the name as if he had never heard of it. 'You said he's your father. If that's so then why ain't you been around before this?'

'I left home five years ago, and only heard a few days ago that there was trouble. So tell me what you're doing here and what's happened to my father.'

'Your old man sold out and left this range. And don't ask me where he went because I ain't got no idea. I was brung in and hired to run the place – keep strangers off.'

'So who hired you?'

'That ain't any of your damn business. Now you better get outa here. If you got any more damn fool questions then ride into town and talk to the sheriff.'

'I'm asking you the questions, and you'd better speak up pretty damn quick. I'm mighty short on patience, Nolan, and you're pushing me over the edge, mister.'

'So what are you gonna do about it?'

Lew gazed impassively at Nolan. He drew a deep breath, fighting down his rising anger as he stepped down from his saddle. He kept the muzzle of his pistol lined up on Nolan's chest, trailed his reins, and stepped up on to the porch. He reached out his left arm and placed his hand in the centre of Nolan's chest, pushing hard. Nolan went backwards a couple of quick steps to keep his balance and then lunged forward, both hands lifting to grapple with Lew, but Lew's pistol swung in a tight arc and the long barrel crashed against Nolan's left temple.

Nolan halted as if he had run into a wall. He stared into Lew's face with hatred and anger mingled in his gaze. Then his eyes blanked out and his knees gave way. He dropped to the porch and remained as if in prayer. Lew

11

lifted his left leg, thrust his foot against Nolan's chest and sent him over backwards. Nolan's head struck the front wall of the house and he relaxed into unconsciousness.

Lew holstered his pistol, grasped Nolan by his shirt collar, and dragged him off the porch and across the yard to the well. When he was released, Nolan lay like a sack of potatoes, breathing heavily, his eyes closed. Lew dropped the bucket into the well, let it fill, and then winched it up. He threw half the contents of the bucket into Nolan's face and watched him splutter back to his senses. Nolan shook his head before looking up, eyes squinting against the afternoon sun. Lew threw the rest of the water into his already streaming face, and the big man bellowed and scrambled unsteadily to his feet.

'Are you ready to talk now?' Lew demanded.

'Go to hell!'

Lew smiled, slid his right foot forward, and threw a right-hand punch as he shifted his weight to his right hip. His knuckles connected solidly with Nolan's jaw with a satisfying crack and Nolan went down again, twisting to land on his face in the dust. He snuffled like a hog in mud, mustered his strength, and then pushed himself unsteadily to his feet, his breathing ragged and laborious.

'I can keep this up all day,' Lew observed, 'but how long can you take it?'

Nolan saw that Lew had holstered his pistol and hurled himself forward with a cry of rage. Lew sidestepped and struck with his left and right fists in two shrewd punches. Nolan finished on his face in the dust again, and this time he remained inert, his breath rasping in his throat.

'It would be easier for you to answer my questions,' Lew

observed. 'If you're still of a mind not to then get up and I'll continue.'

'Get the hell outa here,' Nolan rasped. 'The next time I see you I'll throw lead.'

'If you want to try your luck with a gun then climb on your feet and we'll get to it,' Lew told him. 'I ain't finished yet. I wanta know who hired you, and while you're at it, tell me who bought this place.'

'I don't know the answer to that. The hiring was done by Casey Mitchell, who runs the big saloon in Bostock.'

'So why couldn't you tell me that in the first place?' Lew turned and walked back to the porch. He picked up Nolan's rifle and worked the mechanism until the magazine was empty, threw the long gun off the side of the porch, and then took up his reins and swung into his saddle. He looked at Nolan, who was sitting up by the well, shaking his head, and walked towards the gate. He rode out of the yard and made for the little cow town of Bostock, ten miles to the south.

Lew's thoughts were like quicksilver as he rode. He could not believe his father had sold up and pulled out, especially after writing that letter. Frank Harper had never ducked a fight in his life, and nothing could make him run. And where was his younger brother Wayne? Frank had not mentioned him in the letter, and as far as Lew knew, his brother had remained at the ranch to help work it with his father. Wayne loved cowpunching as much as Lew hated it.

From time to time Lew glanced back, looking for signs of Nolan, but his back trail remained deserted, and he pushed on for Bostock at a fast clip. It was late afternoon

13

when he first spotted the town, and sighed with relief as he rode into the main street.

Nothing seemed to have changed over the past five years, Lew decided. Bostock was a typical cow town, purely functional and geared solely to the wants and needs of local cattlemen. The wide, dusty main street ran north to south, coming from nowhere and heading into anonymity in the opposite direction. He headed for the law office, wanting to speak to old Tom Parrish, the county sheriff. He passed the big saloon on his left, and glanced aside to rake it with his intent gaze, for Nolan said he had been hired to take care of Circle H by Casey Mitchell, who ran the establishment. He noticed a couple of men sitting on chairs on the sidewalk in front of the saloon, and was aware of their unblinking gaze watching his progress along the street.

Lew wondered what had happened to Pete Donovan, who used to own the saloon. He shook his head, aware that places never changed, only the folks in them. He reined in at the hitch rail in front of the law office and stepped down from the saddle, wrapped his reins around the rail, and crossed the sidewalk to enter the office. He paused on the threshold, frowning, his eyes temporarily bemused by the gloomy interior after the strong afternoon sunlight, and looked around. Again, nothing seemed to have changed. The old paper-littered desk was still at the back of the long room, but there was a stranger seated at it that looked up as Lew's spurs tinkled. Lew saw a sheriff's star pinned to the man's shirt front.

'What can I do for you, stranger?' the sheriff demanded, getting to his feet and coming forward from the desk. He was a big man, young, no more than thirty, with a dour expression on his hard face. His blue eyes were filled with question, and something more, which Lew could not read. He was tall and heavily built, wearing a black town suit and a white shirt with a black string tie at his neck. A cartridge belt was buckled around his slender waist and his holster, containing a well-worn Colt .45, was tied down to facilitate a fast draw.

'Where's Sheriff Parrish?' Lew demanded. 'It's him I wanta see.'

'Hey, Parrish retired three years gone. I'm Buck Shenton. I've been handling the law around this county for a couple of years now. What's on your mind, mister? You got some trouble?'

'I'm no stranger,' Lew responded. 'I'm Lew Harper. My father owns the Circle H ranch out at Dead Horse Creek. I'm just back from Montana, and when I reached the ranch a feller by the name of Cleaver Nolan told me my pa had sold up and pulled out three years ago.'

'That's the story as I heard it,' Shenton said. 'It happened before I took over here. How'd you find Nolan? He ain't taken much by strangers showing up on that spread.'

'He wasn't friendly. I had to persuade him to tell me what he was doing on the ranch when I was expecting to find my father there.'

Shenton's gaze sharpened. 'Say, you didn't get rough with Nolan, did you?' he demanded.

'Anything I did was in self-defence. If my father sold Circle H, can you tell me who bought it?'

'There's no *if* about it, Harper.' Shenton shook his head.

'There is in my mind.' Lew suppressed a sigh and made

an effort to contain his impatience. 'Nolan said my father sold up and cleared out three years ago. If that's the case then how come I got a letter from my pa a couple of weeks ago telling me he'd got bad trouble and needed my help at the ranch? Obviously there's something going on that I need to know about.'

A frown appeared on Shenton's face. He shook his head and his tone hardened. 'I'm telling you your father hasn't been around here in the time I've been handling the law. So are you calling me a liar?'

'That doesn't come into it.' Lew reached into his breast pocket and produced the letter. He handed it to Shenton, who read it slowly, his lips moving silently. When he had finished, the sheriff looked into Lew's eyes.

'Is this your father's handwriting?' he demanded.

'I didn't check. It's signed Frank Harper. I had no reason to doubt it was from my father. Let me take another look.' Lew took the letter and scrutinized it closely. The pencil scrawl was faint, and he could not remember his father's handwriting. 'I can't say for sure,' he mused. 'But if it ain't from my pa then who is it from? And who would write to me like this if it wasn't him?'

'I got no idea. There don't seem to be any sense in it.' Shenton shook his head. 'I reckon you better walk soft around here until you do get the lowdown on what it's all about. And don't go throwing your weight around until you've got the rights of it. The best place you can start asking about this is at the bank. Abe Fenner would have handled the sale of the spread, I guess. If you have roughed up Cleaver Nolan and he makes a complaint against you then I reckon you'll be in trouble with the law, which means I'll be breathing down your neck.'

Lew ignored the threat. 'I've got a younger brother – Wayne. Is he around?'

'I ain't seen hide nor hair of him in the time I've been here, but I have heard stories. He got into a shooting scrape about three years ago and was shot bad, so they say. A bullet hit him in the head. It should have killed him but he lived, but when he recovered he couldn't remember a thing about his past, and was sent somewhere east for medical treatment. The bullet scrambled his brains, they say. Go talk to Doc Allen – he might help.'

'Who shot my brother?'

'I couldn't say. Like I said, it happened before my time. All I know is that it was over some gal.'

Lew shook his head. He felt as if he had walked into a nightmare. None of what he had learned seemed to ring true. If his father had left the county three years ago, after selling up, then who had written the letter he had received in Montana only a couple of weeks ago?

'Sorry I can't be of more help,' Shenton said. 'Go on and ask around; see if you can learn anything, but when you've done that I suggest you head back to where you came from and forget about this place.'

Lew stifled a sigh. 'Are you kidding?' he demanded. 'Would you forget about your father if you were in my boots? Hell, I'll go through this town like a blue norther to get at the truth, you can bet. If anything bad has happened to my pa I'll put a kink in the tail of who's done it, and there ain't no two ways about that.'

'You have my sympathy, Harper, but understand this. If you step out of line then I'll slam you behind bars so fast your feet won't touch the ground. Do I make myself clear? If you tread on anyone's toes then you'll face charges.'

'One last question,' Lew said. 'Who owns Circle H right now?'

'I can't answer that.' Shenton suppressed a sigh. 'I don't know a thing about any of this, but I'll be watching you pretty damn close from now on.'

Lew turned, and his boots thudded on the wooden floor as he went to the door. He paused on the sidewalk and looked around the wide street. Nothing seemed to have changed in the past five years, but he had a bad feeling that much had happened beneath the surface of town life, and none of it seemed good.

He climbed into his saddle and rode along the street to the livery barn. There was a water trough outside the big double doors, and he dismounted and allowed his horse to drink. He looked around again as he waited for the animal to take its fill, shaking his head in disbelief at what he had learned. The town looked peaceful enough, as had the Circle H ranch, but something was seriously wrong beneath the apparent calm. Nolan, out at the spread, was a violent man, and Lew wondered about the rider of the white horse, who had disappeared so quickly with Nolan's shots crackling around him. The letter he had received hinted at bad trouble on the range, and he wondered if he had returned too late to take a hand against the trouble-makers.

The horse finished drinking and Lew led it into the barn. He paused on the threshold to look around for the stableman. The interior was gloomy, the corners filled with shadows. A tiny shiver of presentiment trickled along his spine, an integral part of the sixth sense of survival that grew in a man who habitually put his life at risk in the line of duty, and as he became aware of it he dived sideways to the ground and reached for his gun. A split second later the heavy silence was rent asunder by the booming crash of gunfire, and he realized, as he lifted his gun, that the trouble that had apparently enveloped his father was inevitably reaching out for him. . . .

# TWO

Gunsmoke plumed across the space inside the stable, and the crash of the shooting hammered against Lew's ears. He heard the strike of a bullet slamming into his horse, and rolled aside as the animal squealed in agony and fell to the ground with threshing hoofs. He squirmed to one side, intent on bringing his pistol into play, aware, from the sound of the shooting that at least two guns were firing at him. He had walked into a perfect gun trap, and wondered, if it had been set for him personally, how his unknown enemies were able to act against him so quickly.

A bullet clipped his left shoulder as he raised himself slightly to take in the situation. He saw the flash of a gun coming from a stall to his right and sent two probing shots into the area before looking for the second ambusher. He heard a thin cry of pain beneath the bluster of shots as he eased around to try and pinpoint the second gun. He saw a movement over by the door to the stableman's office, followed by the flash of a pistol. A slug snarled in his right ear and he triggered a shot in reply before moving again, rolling aside quickly. Bullets thudded around him but he was not touched, and kept shooting until the hammer of his gun clicked on an empty cartridge.

He ducked, hastily dragged cartridges from his belt, broke the gun, and thumbed in fresh loads. By the time he was ready to continue, the ambushers had ceased firing and a silence was descending over the barn, an uneasy silence marred by the fading echoes of the shooting. He heard the sound of running feet at the rear of the stable, and then there was nothing except drifting gunsmoke. His attackers had fled.

Lew got cautiously to his feet. His ears were ringing, his nostrils irritated by pungent gunsmoke. He took a deep breath and looked around. His horse was dead – shot through the chest. He heaved a sigh, wondering where the stableman was. He was hair-triggered for more action, and ran to the back door of the barn to look out across the back lots. But his attackers had gone. They had struck like snakes, and pulled out when they realized they could not succeed, evidently afraid of being seen, which could mean they were local and recognizable. He wondered what the local set-up was and how it had involved his father in the first place.

He walked back to where his horse was lying, and heard a voice calling from outside. He recognized Shenton's voice, and answered quickly. The sheriff came striding into the barn, his pistol in his hand and inquiry on his tanned features.

'What the hell happened here?' he demanded.

'I sure wish I had the answer to that,' replied Lew, and explained briefly.

'There were two of 'em, huh?' Shenton nodded. 'Did

you hit either of them?'

'I reckon I did.' Lew remembered the cry of pain he had heard, and the thought started up a painful throbbing in his left shoulder where he had been caught. He lifted his right hand to his shoulder, found a tear in his shirt, and felt blood dribbling from where he had been nicked by a bullet. He shrugged the shoulder experimentally and was relieved when it moved easily, with no grating of a broken bone. 'They took out the back way,' he added.

'Let's take a look.' Shenton went quickly between the stalls to the back door and Lew followed closely. 'Two sets of boot tracks in the dust,' Shenton observed. 'They look like they've just been made. Let's see if we can track them.'

Lew pulled his gun, checked its loads, and returned it to his holster. Shenton glanced at him but said nothing. They followed the boot tracks along the back lots and into the nearest alley, where they disappeared on hard ground. Shenton kept going to the end of the alley, and looked out to check the street. Lew joined him. He saw the street was practically deserted, except for curious men hurrying towards the livery barn.

'Did you get a good look at either man?' Shenton demanded.

'No.' Lew shook his head. 'They cut loose at me when I entered the barn, and I hit cover fast. Then there was a lot of gunsmoke, and they were gone before I realized it.'

'I haven't seen any strangers around town,' Shenton mused, 'so it's got to be the work of locals.' His eyes were shrewd as he looked into Lew's face. 'Did anyone know you were coming back?' he demanded.

'Not a soul.' Lew paused, and added: 'Except whoever

wrote me that letter.'

'You don't think it was your father?'

'Not if he left here three years ago.'

'So if no one knew you were coming back then no one could have been waiting for you to show up here.'

'That's how I see it.'

'Why would anyone but your father want you to come back? And why would he want you back if he wasn't living here? He would have asked you to return to where he's living right now, wouldn't he?'

'That's one of the things I intend to look into,' Lew said firmly.

'And you walked straight into a gun trap,' Shenton added. 'That doesn't make any sense at all. How could anyone set a trap for you without knowing you were coming?'

Lew was looking around the street as they talked. His gaze rested on the front of the saloon, and he recalled the two men that had been sitting outside when he arrived. It had crossed his mind then that they had taken an undue interest in him as he passed them, but had discarded the thought because they could not have known who he was. The only person he had talked to was Nolan. He relayed that fact to Shenton, and mentioned the two men.

'We've got nothing else to go on,' Shenton said instantly. 'As far as I know Nolan ain't come into town, so let's check out them two fellers. They probably followed everyone to the livery barn so we'll ask about them in the saloon before we brace them.'

Lew followed Shenton into the saloon, which was deserted except for an old man standing behind the bar who was tall and thin, and as bald as a coot. His dark eyes narrowed when he looked up and saw Shenton, and his mouth pulled into a thin line. His shirt sleeves were rolled up to the elbows and he was wearing a white apron that had seen better days.

'I reckoned you'd be checking up on that shooting I heard a while ago, Sheriff,' he declared.

'That is what I am doing, Casey,' Shenton replied. 'This here is Lew Harper, whose father used to run Circle H. This is Casey Mitchell, Harper, the owner of this watering hole. There were two men sitting on your seats outside the saloon some minutes ago, Casey. You got any idea who they were?'

'I don't keep an eye on those seats,' Mitchell replied. 'Anyone in town is free to use them, and they don't have to come in here to ask permission. Can you describe the two in question?'

Lew thought for a moment. 'They were range dressed. I think one of them was wearing a blue shirt. He was kind of large, and had the brim of his Stetson pinned up at the front. I don't remember anything about the other one.'

'They came in here for a drink an hour ago,' Mitchell said. 'I remember the pinned-back hat. Not many punchers wear their hats like that. They were strangers, and only had the one drink before leaving. I didn't know they were sitting outside. Do you reckon they were involved in the shooting?'

'We're gonna find out,' Shenton said.

Lew wanted to ask Mitchell about the hiring of Cleaver Nolan out at Circle H, but did not want to broach the subject in front of Shenton. He was aware that Mitchell was staring at him, and wondered if there was anything significant in the saloon man's interest. He meant to find out, and planned to revisit Mitchell later. Shenton walked to the batwings, paused, and looked back at Lew.

'Are you coming?' he demanded.

Lew hurried after him and they went along the street back to the livery barn. A crowd of about twenty townsmen was standing in and around the entrance, and Shenton shouted at them to back off. A small man dressed in a long brown dust coat was standing beside Lew's dead horse, and he swung round when he heard the sound of the sheriff's voice.

'I can't leave this place for ten minutes without something bad happening,' he declared. 'Whose horse is this, and what was all that shooting about?'

'That's what we're trying to find out,' Shenton said. 'Ed, this is Lew Harper – lived at Circle H until five years ago. This is Ed Faylen, Harper. He's another who moved here after you left.'

'Howdy do, Harper? So what happened here? Who shot your horse?'

Lew explained, and described the men they were looking for.

'I saw them,' Faylen said. 'They rode out just as I got back; they went out the back door in a tearing hurry.'

Shenton ran through the barn to the back door and peered out. He turned immediately and came hurrying back to a stall, entered, and started saddling a powerful black.

'I can see them in the distance,' Shenton said as he slapped a saddle on the black. 'I'll go fetch them.'

'You'll need help,' Lew said instantly. 'I'll ride with you if I can borrow a horse.'

'You look like you need to see Doc Allen,' Shenton commented. 'I can handle this. Go get yourself fixed up and wait until I come back.'

Lew knew by the tone in Shenton's voice that the sheriff would not let him ride along so he nodded and left the barn. Townsmen were still coming towards the stable from the main street, and he passed them without answering their questions. He saw no one he knew, and was faintly surprised at the number of strangers who had moved into the town during the past five years.

The layout of the town had not changed at all. Lew knew where Doc Allen resided, found the doctor standing in his doorway fronting the street. He had heard the shooting and was wondering if anyone needed his help. Allen was a tall, thin man with a lined and weathered face and kindly blue eyes. He stared at Lew intently, his eyes showing that he did not readily recognize him.

'I'm Lew Harper, Doc,' Lew said. 'How you been these past five years?'

'Lew Harper?' Allen peered intently into Lew's face and then nodded. 'You've sure done a powerful lot of growing up since I last saw you, son. I could have passed you in the street without knowing you.'

'And you don't look a day older than when I last saw you, Doc,' Lew replied.

'You're bleeding. Were you caught up in that shooting?'

'I sure was.' Lew explained what happened, and went on to talk of his return to the Circle H. When he mentioned receiving a letter from his father only two weeks before, Allen frowned and shook his head.

'That's mighty strange, Lew. Did Frank write as if he was still at the ranch?'

'Sure he did, although he didn't say so in as many words. Here, read the letter for yourself.'

He produced the letter and Allen scanned it quickly, and then looked around the street as he folded it and returned it to the envelope.

'Lew, you'd better come inside and I'll take a look at your shoulder. This is mighty strange. Frank sold up just after Wayne was shot. That would be a little over three years ago. I don't know how Wayne managed to survive, but he did, and he needed special treatment so I arranged for him to go Kansas City. That's partly why Frank sold up. He needed money for Wayne's treatment and wanted to be near your brother while he was on the mend. I mentioned your name at the time, and reckoned Frank would contact you.'

'He didn't, Doc,' Lew said. 'He must have been still sore at me for leaving home.'

'But Wayne was lying at death's door for weeks,' Allen said. 'You should have been notified.'

They entered the house and Allen led the way into his office. He sat Lew down in a chair by the window and opened his shirt. Lew bore his ministrations stoically.

'So you know Pa and Wayne got away from here, huh?' Lew said at length. 'Then where did this letter come from? It was posted here in Bostock. Who in hell sent it? And why didn't Pa get in touch with me when Wayne was shot? That's the least he could have done.'

'I take it that you didn't write home regularly,' Allen observed.

'Well, no. Pa didn't like the idea of me going off like I did, and I reckoned to make good in Montana before coming back to see him.' Lew shook his head. 'I wish now I had been more reasonable. How did Wayne come to be shot? The new sheriff told me he got into an argument with a man over some girl. Is that a fact?'

'That's exactly what happened. Wayne started seeing Jane Wishart. Her father Joe owns the Box W, if you remember.'

'Yeah, I remember.' Lew nodded.

'Do you recall Jack Tate? I reckon you should. He was a bully, and I remember you whaling the tar outa him one Saturday night right there on the street in front of the saloon.'

'I recall the incident.'

'Well, Tate got interested in Jane about the time Wayne started seeing her. Tate didn't like the competition and started bullying Wayne, until your brother turned on him. Wayne did a good job, too. I remember patching up Tate afterwards. He spent a week in bed to get over his injuries. But when he got up again he took a gun to Wayne – never gave your brother a chance. He shot Wayne in the head from behind. I thought Wayne was dead when he was carried in here, but the bullet caught him a glancing blow and he survived, although he was good for nothing when he got on his feet again. I reckoned his only chance of regaining a useful life was to see one of those medical specialists back east, and Frank took my advice. He sold up and moved out.'

'Did you hear from Pa again?'

Doc Allen shook his head and spoke wistfully. 'No. I

guess he was too busy looking after Wayne to have any time for old friends.'

Lew was silent for a moment, his thoughts bitter. Then he sighed. 'I sure wish I had known about this,' he mused. 'What happened to Jack Tate?'

'He went to prison for five years. The last I heard of him he tried an unsuccessful escape and received another two years on his original sentence.'

Doc Allen finished his ministrations and Lew got to his feet. 'You could do worse than ride out to Box W and talk to Jane Wishart,' he mused. 'It was always Wayne she was fond of, and she's never looked at another man in the time he's been away. She might have heard from your father over the years, and could even know where he is at right now.'

'Thanks, Doc, I'll look Jane up when I get the time. I've one or two things to take care of right now, but I'll get around to seeing her.'

'Just watch your back, huh? There's trouble in the county, especially around here, and it looks like you've been caught up in it.'

'What kind of trouble, Doc?'

'It's difficult to pin down, especially with so many new men around these days. We knew where we stood when Parrish was the sheriff. This new man, Shenton, seems to handle the job well enough, but it's not the same as it was. There's trouble, OK? You have to look hard at the situation to see any kind of a pattern. I have, because I get around a lot in this job, and people talk. They tell me things a sheriff would never hear of. And I reckon it'll get worse before it gets better.'

'I'll look into it now I'm back,' Lew promised. 'Right now, I wanta have a word with Casey Mitchell.'

'Do you think he's got a hand in what's going on?' Doc Allen's eyes filled with speculation.

Lew grimaced, 'I was a deputy sheriff in Montana for the last three years, and I learned a lot about law work. I'll check right through the whole business until I get a picture in my mind. When I dropped by Circle H before coming into town I ran up against Cleaver Nolan. He didn't want to talk, and he's a real bully of a man, but I got him to open up, and he mentioned that Casey Mitchell hired him to take care of the spread. I want to know what Mitchell's stake is in this.'

'Be careful, Lew,' Allen's craggy face showed a grim expression. 'There are some mighty hard cases hanging out in that saloon.'

Lew shrugged and took his leave. He had to play it as it came, and trust to his gun speed to keep him out of trouble. It certainly looked as if someone was playing for big stakes, and he had been drawn into the game without being aware of the rules. He went back along the street to the saloon and pushed through the batwings. Some of the men who had been drawn to the livery barn by the shooting were now lined up at the bar, and Casey Mitchell was busy serving drinks. Lew paused for a moment at the end of the bar, listening to the buzz of conversation, and watching the saloon man. Shortly, Mitchell came along the bar to where Lew was waiting.

'What'll it be?' he demanded. There was a fine sheen of sweat on his forehead.

'A beer,' Lew replied, 'and maybe you can answer a

30

question that's bothering me.'

'Try me.' Mitchell moved away, poured a beer, and returned to set it in front of Lew, who slapped a silver dollar on the bar top.

'First one's on the house.' Mitchell pushed the coin away. 'What's the question?'

Lew explained his visit to Circle H and meeting Cleaver Nolan. Mitchell raised his eyebrows, and then grinned.

'Knowing Nolan as I do, I'm surprised you ain't covered in bruises,' he commented. 'I picked him to work out there because of his unfriendly manner.'

'Nolan is the one that collected the bruises.' Lew smiled at the memory. 'He was reluctant to talk to me, but finally saw sense and opened up. He said you hired him to take care of Circle H. Do you own the place?'

'Yeah, I do, although it ain't widely known around here. I bought it when it came up for sale. I wasn't the only one after it, as a matter of fact, but it came to me. The business was done through the bank so you can check with Abe Fenner for the details.'

'Are you running cows out there?'

'Sure I am. That's why I bought the spread.'

'Is Nolan alone out there, running it single-handed?'

'The hell he is! I got a crew of four punchers out there. They handle the stock. Nolan just keeps an eye on the place. He sure ain't a cow nurse.'

'Are you having any trouble on the range?'

'There is some trouble around – always is on cattle range – a bit of rustling, arguments over water rights and boundaries. You know how it is. You've lived on a ranch. But with the men I got working for me I don't expect to find trouble. They can handle most things that crop up. Does that answer your question?'

'Yeah, I guess so.' Lew straightened up and drank his beer. He was parched, and the liquid lubricated his throat.

Mitchell began to move away but paused. 'How come you found trouble here in town? Do you know the men who ambushed you or did they follow you from Montana?'

'How'd you know I've come from Montana?'

Mitchell shrugged. 'News soon gets around. Excuse me; I've got work to do.'

Lew finished his beer and watched Mitchell serving customers. He was not satisfied with what he had learned, and suspected that something was not quite right with the apparent situation. He wondered how Shenton was doing on the trail of the two bushwhackers, and it crossed his mind that they could be some of the crew Mitchell had working at the Circle H. Nolan had been the only man in the county who knew he had returned, and he could have set two of the men to track him from the ranch and shoot him down. He felt a fluttering of tension unfold in his mind, and began to wish he had ignored Shenton's order to stick around town and had accompanied the lawman.

He left the saloon with the feeling that he had not learned anything worthwhile. The sun was now way over into the western half of the sky, and he became aware that he had not eaten since early morning. He headed for the diner next to the general store and entered for a meal. It was too early for the evening rush and he had the place almost to himself. He sat down at a small table and eventually a waitress appeared and approached him. He recognized her. She was Molly, the daughter of the owner,

Dick Morris, and she had been a waitress in the diner long before Lew had left the ranch.

'Hi, Molly,' he greeted. 'Long time no see. How's life been treating you?'

She gazed at him in surprise, and it took her several seconds to get his name.

'Well, I do declare! It's Lew Harper, no less! This is a surprise, Lew. I never expected to see you again. I thought you'd gone for good. What brings you back after so long?'

'It's family business, Molly.' He replied.

'But your family doesn't live here any more. They've been gone three years now – upped and left after Wayne was shot. . . .'

Molly's voice trailed off and she shook her head. She was tall and slender, aged about thirty, Lew guessed. Her face was long and she was plain and unattractive. Her dark brown hair was straight and cut to just above her shoulders. She had brown eyes that seemed dull and uninterested in her surroundings, and Lew could understand that for she had been a waitress, at the beck and call of every diner, for as long as he could remember. He glanced at her left hand and noted the absence of a wedding ring.

'I heard about Wayne,' he said. 'Do you have any idea where he and Pa moved to when they left?'

'Back east is all I can tell you.' She shook her head. 'It was a bad business all round, and no one knew they were pulling out until after they had gone. Such a pity! Wayne was a lovely young man. Have you come back for good or will you be moving on again?'

'I can't say at the moment.' He shook his head. 'It

depends on what I find out.'

'Is there trouble?' She looked pointedly at the blood-stain on the left shoulder of his shirt. 'I heard shooting some time ago. Were you caught up in that?'

'I think I was mistaken for someone else.' Lew did not like the direction the conversation was taking and changed the subject. 'What have you got to eat? I've had nothing since breakfast before sunup this morning.'

She took his order and hurried off into the kitchen. Lew tried to relax, but his head was whirling with thought and conjecture, and foremost in his mind was a stark question: What had he walked into on his return, and where did he go from here?

# THREE

Buck Shenton galloped out of town on the trail of the two ambushers and rapidly overhauled them. They were not travelling fast, for one of them was hung over in his saddle, his chest stained with blood. His face was pale and he was only semi-conscious. Shenton cursed under his breath when he neared them, and increased his speed. They heard his hoof beats, and the unwounded man, leading his companion's horse, twisted in his saddle, recognized the newcomer, and reined in. Shenton arrived and pulled up in a cloud of dust. Sunlight glinted on his law star.

'What the hell were you and Buster up to, Miller?' Shenton demanded. 'Ain't you got the sense you was born with, attacking Harper in town in broad daylight?'

'It was Nolan sent us out after him,' Miller protested, shrugging his thin shoulders. 'Harper rode into the ranch and started throwing his weight about. He asked questions, and laid into Nolan until he gave out some answers. Anyway, we beat Harper into town and I saw Casey, who said to nail Harper when he showed up. So it was OK, Casey being the boss.'

'And you made a mess of it,' Shenton observed. 'Harper was all for coming out and finishing you off. All you've done is given him something to think about. How bad is Buster? He's gonna die, I hope?'

'He's hit bad, and I reckon he will die if we don't get a doc out to him.'

'You can't do that.' Shenton shook his head. 'See what you can for him, and if he dies you'll have to bury him out on the prairie where he won't be found.'

'What about Harper?' Miller demanded.

'I'll watch him; it looks like I'll have to take care of him myself if he starts poking around. Tell Nolan I'm not pleased with him. He's getting too big for his boots. And I'll talk to Casey when I get back to town. He's beginning to work on taking over the ranch next to Harper's, the Box W, and he needs to handle it better than the Circle H was taken. But like I told him, he should bring in some men with plenty of savvy instead of hiring scum like you.'

'We were only doing what we get paid for,' Miller protested, the expression on his hard face revealing that he was not happy with Shenton's description of him. 'It was Nolan called the wrong shots. You got no call to talk to me like that. I reckon we don't get enough pay for what we're doing, anyway.'

'You didn't kill Harper,' Shenton snarled, 'and you shouldn't have tried for him in the middle of the damn town in broad daylight. If you're not satisfied with your wages then take it up with Mitchell. Get moving now, head back to the ranch, and lie low. I'll ride back and tell Harper I lost your tracks in that rocky stretch this side of Dead Horse Creek. Keep to rough ground between here and the spread so you won't leave too many fresh tracks.'

Miller muttered under his breath and kicked his horse into motion. Shenton watched him until the two horses were out of sight. Then he heaved a sigh and shook his head before turning his mount to ride back to town. . . .

With a good meal inside him, Lew felt better able to begin the task of checking on the two ambushers. He walked back to the stable to find his dead horse had been removed from the stable entrance. He went to the back door of the barn and found the liveryman, Ed Faylen, standing in the corral with two townsmen. Faylen came to confront him.

'I've got rid of your horse,' he said, 'and put your gear in my office. You'll want another horse now, I guess, huh?'

'I'd rather rent than buy,' Lew told him. 'Have you got a mount with some life in it?'

'I ain't gonna rent an animal to you if it's likely to get shot,' Faylen said.

'OK, so sell me one. I need to ride out to Box W. Let's do a deal right now. The sooner I get out of town the better I'll like it.'

'I'll show you what I've got.' Faylen led the way into the barn.

Faylen was a sharp horse dealer, and Lew had no option but to buy another mount. He picked a chestnut that sounded like it had no problems with its breathing and looked as if it could run to the end of the street without falling down. He put his gear on the animal and rode out immediately, intent on visiting the Wishart ranch. He had in his mind an image of the unknown rider on the white horse that had galloped away from Cleaver Nolan, aware that the rider had headed out on the trail to Box W.

Lew left the barn by the rear door and checked the dust on the back lots for signs of fresh tracks. He found the prints of two horses, decided they had been left by his ambushers, and dismounted to examine them. He studied them intently until he was satisfied he would be able to recognize them anywhere, and then continued out of town, deciding to ride to Box W because it was too late in the day to track the ambushers.

'The sun had disappeared beyond the western horizon when Lew reined up and looked at the lights of the Wishart ranch. He remembered the place well, for he had been friendly with Jane Wishart before he left for Montana. Shadows had closed in and stars were glimmering remotely in the sky when he entered the ranch yard. The breeze blowing into his face had cooled considerably. The porch was in almost complete darkness, and a harsh voice called to him from the shadows as he prepared to dismount.

'Who are you?' the voice demanded.

'Is that you, Joe?' Lew demanded. 'I'm Lew Harper.'

He heard an exclamation from the porch, and the sound of someone getting off a chair. Then a tall man stepped forward into the yellow lamplight issuing from a front window of the house, and Lew recognized Joe Wishart.

'Lew Harper?' Wishart said. 'The hell you say! Hey, I'm mighty glad to see you, son. You've been in my thoughts a lot lately. Get down and come into the house. What brings you back at this time?'

Lew dismounted and tethered his horse to a post. He

stepped up on to the porch and gripped Wishart's outstretched hand.

'It's good to see you, Lew,' Wishart said warmly. 'It's a pity you ever went away. Your pa had a lot of trouble three years ago and he could have done with you at his side.'

'Three years ago?' Lew frowned and lifted a hand to his breast pocket where he kept the letter purporting to come from his father. 'I had a letter from Pa a couple of weeks ago saying he was getting trouble. That's why I'm here. I know nothing about what happened three years ago.'

'Frank wrote you from here?' Wishart sounded surprised.

'That's right.' Lew produced the letter.

Wishart took it and walked to the window to read it by lamplight. Lew stood motionless, waiting for Wishart's reaction. The rancher came back to him.

'Frank ain't been around here since he took your brother Wayne back east to see one of them fancy doctors. He sold out three years ago because he needed the money for Wayne's treatment in Kansas City.'

'I've spoken to Doc Allen. He told me to come here and talk to Jane.'

'Well, come on into the house and we'll talk.' Wishart turned to the front door, opened it, and lamplight shafted out. He placed a hand on Lew's shoulder and pushed him gently into the doorway. Lew entered the house, and as he paused on the threshold he felt a lightning strike of pain in his left thigh. His leg let him down, and, as he sprawled on the floor, he heard the report of a distant rifle throwing echoes across the yard.

Wishart dived into the room and slammed the door. He

39

dropped to one knee beside Lew, his face twisted by shock.

'Are you hit bad, Lew?' he demanded.

'I'll live, I guess,' Lew said through gritted teeth. 'Are you getting trouble?'

'It hadn't come to shooting before you showed up.' Wishart crossed the room to the big fireplace and lifted a Winchester off the wall above it. 'You stay down while I take a look outside. Jane's upstairs. I reckon she'll be down if she heard that shot.'

'I was ambushed in Bostock earlier,' Lew said. 'It's my fight, Joe. Let me go out there.'

'Anyone shooting up this place is my business,' Wishart growled. 'I'll go out the back door and circle the house. Stay put, Lew.'

Lew struggled into a sitting position and examined his leg. There was a tear in the left leg of his pants some three inches above the knee. Blood was seeping through the fabric and he took out his pocket knife and slit the material to bare the wound. Relief filled him when he found it was not serious. At that moment the inner door opened and Jane Wishart came running into the room. She paused and gazed at Lew as if she could not believe her eyes, and then hurried to his side.

'Lew, I'm glad to see you,' she said, dropping to her knees beside him. 'What's going on? I heard a shot.'

'I don't know who fired it, but he was aiming at me,' Lew replied. 'This is the second time today I've been set up as a target.'

'I'll get some water and a bandage,' Jane said.

Lew looked at her as she arose. She was tall and had grown some in the past five years. She had always been an

40

attractive girl, and her early twenties bore out the promise of her youth. But her face was marred by anxiety as she paused and turned to face him.

'Where's Pa?' she demanded. 'He was sitting on the porch when I went upstairs.'

'He was out there when I arrived,' he replied. 'I was shot as he was bringing me into the house. He took his rifle and went out the back door to take a look around.'

'Then we'll leave him to handle that chore,' she said.

Lew tried to relax. He listened intently for the sound of more shooting but now a tense silence hung over the ranch. Jane returned with a bowl of water and some cloths. She bent over his leg and examined the wound before bathing it.

'It's a flesh wound,' she said, greatly relieved. She glanced at the bloodstain on his left shoulder and pursed her lips. 'So you've been shot twice today! Let's hope there won't be a third time.'

She bandaged the wound and then wrapped a cloth around his thigh to cover the tear in his pants.

'That will hold you until you can get to Doc Allen,' she observed.

'Doc told me to talk to you.' Lew looked keenly at her. 'What happened three years ago when Wayne was shot? Doc Allen said Jack Tate shot Wayne because of you.'

'That's what most people think.' Jane frowned. Her dark eyes seemed to be staring into the past. 'But Wayne was never interested in me, and as far as I was concerned there was only one man in the county who ever had my attention.'

'Who was that?' Lew demanded.

41

'It doesn't matter now.' She shook her head and smiled wistfully. 'He went away and never wrote to me or came back. It was as if I never existed in his life, or that he never ever gave a single thought to me.

'So what happened to Wayne?' Lew's mind was overloaded with the problem that had brought him back from Montana.

'You'd better talk to him about that.' Jane sighed. 'It's not a pleasant story.'

'I don't know where he is,' he replied. 'I wish I could talk to him.'

'He's here now, with us. He showed up about six weeks ago – came walking into the yard while me and Pa were sitting on the porch one sundown. He's got a bad scar on his head where Tate's bullet hit him, and he couldn't tell us much. He doesn't remember a thing about what happened to him after he was shot. It seems the incident was wiped out of his mind by Jack Tate's bullet. All we could get out of him was that a part of the memory of his former life returned to him recently and he came west looking for some answers. He knows he has a brother – the doctors told him about you.'

Lew frowned at her words, shaking his head slowly. 'So where is my pa?' he demanded. 'How come he let Wayne travel alone in that condition?'

'Wayne thinks your father is dead – killed when he went missing three years ago. Frank took Wayne east to the doctor's clinic, paid for his treatment, saw Wayne settled in, and then told the doctor he was heading back here to sort out some trouble. But he was never seen around here after he left; and never showed up again back east to see

42

Wayne. The doctor told Wayne some of what had happened in an attempt to restore his memory, and that's why Wayne returned, to try to find out what had happened to your father.'

'Where is Wayne now?' Lew's brain felt as if it had been packed in ice. Shock crawled through him, and his nerve-ends felt raw and shredded.

'He's upstairs. I don't know what happened today. He was out riding on my horse and returned here in a state of shock.'

'What's the colour of your horse?' Lew asked.

'It's a white mare. Why do you ask?'

Lew recalled the rider of a white horse fleeing from Cleaver Nolan's rifle shots. He told Jane of the incident and saw horror fill her gaze.

'So that's where he was. We've told him that the Circle H doesn't belong to your family now but he doesn't accept that. I expect he rode in there looking for your father.'

'So what happened to Frank? I had a letter from him only two weeks ago.'

'No.' Jane shook her head, a sad smile twisting her lips. 'The letter was my idea. I got Wayne to write it because I felt that you should be here to take care of him and try to settle the trouble. Wayne is unable to do anything about it, and if he rides around like he did today it will be only a matter of time before he's killed. It's your responsibility to do something, Lew.'

'It's a pity you didn't write me at the time Wayne was shot,' Lew said slowly. 'I might have been able to do something while Pa was still around. Is there any evidence that he is dead?'

'He hasn't been seen for three years. If he came back here after he settled Wayne back east then he must have walked into big trouble and got himself killed, otherwise he would have been seen. When Wayne showed up we made some inquiries around town, and even checked at the bank. Frank must have had a great deal of money from the sale of Circle H, but Abe Fenner showed us details of your father's bank account, and it seemed his account was closed when he took Wayne east.'

'So he was paid money for the ranch.' Lew gnawed on his bottom lip. 'I understand that Casey Mitchell bought Circle H.'

'Mitchell is not a nice man, Lew. My pa went to talk to him and got short shrift for his pains. Since then, bad things have been happening around here.'

'Like me getting shot tonight,' Lew mused.

'Mitchell told Pa he was ready to buy this place any time Pa felt like selling out, and there are rumours that he bought Bert Sadler and Herb Bean out of their spreads when they got into difficulties with their mortgages.'

'So that's what's going on! A land-grabber is at work, and it looks like Casey Mitchell's behind it.'

Lew broke off and stiffened when he heard a solitary shot out there in the night.

'I'd better get out there and see if your father needs help,' he said, pushing himself to his feet, but a groan escaped him as he put weight on his left leg.

'Don't go.' Jane placed a hand on his arm and gripped it tightly. 'Pa might mistake you in the dark for an intruder, and we don't want any accidents. Just stay put. Pa knows what he's doing.'

Lew sat down again, stuck his left leg out, and gripped it with both hands above the wound to assuage the pain. Jane regarded him with sympathy in her dark eyes.

'I don't know where or how you'll start on this problem,' she mused. 'But there's nothing you can do about Circle H. It's obvious that Mitchell paid your father for the spread.'

'But did he have my father killed afterwards? I was struck by the fact that there are so many new faces around town, and most of them are hardcases. And I don't like Buck Shenton. He hasn't got the look of a lawman about him. What happened to Sheriff Parrish?'

'He had an accident – broke both his legs when his buggy overturned in a storm. And he didn't get over the shock of it so he retired. But Shenton seems to be a good sheriff. He keeps the peace well.'

'How does he get along with Casey Mitchell?'

'It's impossible to tell just by looking at them.'

Boots sounded outside on the porch. Lew palmed his gun. Joe Wishart's voice called.

'I'm coming in. Hold your fire, Lew.'

The front door opened and Wishart entered, screwing up his eyes against the light. He put his Winchester back over the fireplace and turned to face them, his face grim.

'I got a fix on him. He was on the far side of the corral. I was sneaking up on him when his horse whickered. He took out fast, and I fired a shot at him but he kept right on going. I don't think I hit him. It's the hell of a business when a hardcase can ride right into a man's yard and start shooting up the place.'

'Whoever he was, he came for me,' Lew said, 'so you

45

better leave him to me. I'd like to stay here tonight and look around for his tracks in the morning.'

'Sure.' Wishart nodded. 'Stay with us for as long as you want. It might be safer for you to have us backing you. I've got a crew of three men, but they're on a trip at the moment, bringing in fresh stock from Buffalo Crossing. Has Jane told you about Wayne's situation?'

Lew nodded. 'Yeah, and it's not good. What do you think of it?'

'I don't know what to think.' Wishart sighed heavily. 'I don't like the fact that your father hasn't been seen around. We were good friends, and I'd like to think that I'd be the first man he'd turn to if he was in trouble. But he's never showed up, and knowing the kind of man he is, I'm sure he would have made his presence felt if he'd been able to. He would have gone bull-headed for anyone who was giving him trouble.'

'So you think he's dead.' Lew spoke in a flat, unemotional tone, but his mind was seething with conjecture, and the hope that his father just might still be alive.

'It sure looks that way to me,' Wishart said sadly. 'I wish I could think otherwise, but the facts are against Frank still being alive. Three years have passed. He's dead for sure.'

'Come and see Wayne.' Jane got to her feet, her voice breaking the tension. 'He won't know you, of course, and from the way he talks about you he just doesn't understand why you've never shown up around here.'

Lew arose, limped out of the room behind the girl, and followed her up the stairs to a bedroom. She opened a door and Lew entered the room behind her.

'There's someone here to see you, Wayne,' she said,

and stepped aside so Lew could see the young man lying on a bed.

Lew recognized his younger brother instantly. Wayne had grown up in the last five years. He was taller and had filled out, and his face looked much older than his twenty-one years. There were lines on his forehead and his eyes carried the dullness of suffering. The bullet scar on his forehead and left temple was deep; an angry red where no hair grew, and the hair that surrounded the scar was an unnatural white. Lew was appalled when he saw the wound, and wondered how Wayne had managed to survive. Jack Tate had certainly intended to kill him when he fired the shot.

'Wayne, this is your brother Lew,' Jane said softly.

Wayne looked up at Lew. His eyes were dull, with no animation. He shook his head.

'I don't know you,' he said hesitantly. 'Pa told me about you after I'd been shot, but he never said why you didn't come to see us. We were in bad trouble, but you left us to it.'

'That's not true, Wayne,' Lew said strongly. 'I didn't know about the trouble. If I had been aware of it I would have come home right away. Jane got you to write to me a couple of weeks ago, and here I am now, as fast as I could make it. I'm gonna get to the bottom of this trouble, you can bet.'

'It looks like you've been in a fight already,' Wayne observed. 'There's blood on you.'

Lew sat down on the side of the bed. He placed a hand on Wayne's shoulder. Wayne shook his head and looked away, obviously not trusting him.

47

'Can you answer some questions for me, Wayne?' Lew asked.

'I'm not good at questions.' Wayne shook his head. 'I can't keep my thoughts straight. But ask anyway, and I'll do my best.'

'Were you out at Circle H this afternoon, riding a white horse?'

Wayne thought for a few moments, his face screwed up in concentration. Then he nodded.

'Sure. I went to see if they'd seen anything of Pa. When he left me back east he told me he was coming back here to sort out the trouble and would return to get me, but I never saw him again, and Jane tells me that was three years ago. One of the things I can't do is keep track of time.'

'And what happened when you got to the ranch today? Did you see Nolan?'

'I don't know his name. He was a big man. He didn't even listen to what I had to say. He told me I was on private property and he'd shoot me if I didn't leave. I rode off, and he followed and fired at me. I took cover in a stand of trees and fired a couple of shots in his direction before hightailing it out of there.'

'Do you remember anything about being shot in the head by Jack Tate?'

'No. I was told about it later.'

'So you don't know why Tate shot you?'

'I've got no idea. I don't remember Jack Tate, and I'm sure I didn't do anything against him.'

Lew glanced at Jane, who was listening attentively to the questioning.

'What did Tate say at his trial about the shooting?' he

asked her.

'He said it was over a woman. He didn't use my name, but it came out later that I was supposed to be the girl in question, although that is not true. I never liked Tate. I couldn't stand the sight of him. You know what kind of a man he was. I don't think I ever said more than half a dozen words to him in my life.'

'Have you any idea what job Tate was doing at the time of the shooting?'

'He had a job in the saloon as a swamper, as I recall.' Jane frowned. 'Are you thinking Wayne being shot was all part of the trouble?'

'Why else would Tate shoot Wayne? What reason could he have? Did he work for Mitchell before he went to prison, or did Mitchell take over the saloon after Tate was jailed?'

'I seem to remember Tate was working at the saloon when Mitchell came to town and bought the place.' Jane heaved a sigh. 'Tate stayed on until he went to prison. Are you making out a case against Tate and Mitchell? You're talking of things I would never have considered.'

'I was a deputy sheriff in Montana for three years,' Lew said firmly. 'The way I see it, I'm gonna need that experience to try and get to the bottom of what's been going on around here. I came into this situation at the deep end of the pond, but I'm beginning to get a few ideas, and I'll start checking up come morning. But you're going to stay out of this, Wayne. No more riding around on that white horse. You stay here out of sight while I handle the dirty work. I'm more fitted to it.'

'You can count on us for any help you might need,'

Jane said. 'It seems that we're about to be caught up in this bad business, whether we like it or not.'

'I'm sure my pa didn't want trouble,' Lew said grimly. 'I'm gonna find out what happened, you can bet, and everyone who was involved will pay for it, whatever it costs.'

# FOUR

The next morning the sun was barely above the eastern horizon when Lew accompanied Joe Wishart across the yard to the corral of the Box W ranch. He was limping badly; the pain in the wound in his leg had kept him awake for most of the night and his thoughts had plagued him with uncertainty and hopelessness. He felt sure that his father was dead, and he felt responsible for the situation, aware that if he had been around at the time then the worst would not have occurred.

'Here's where that buzzard fired at you,' Wishart said, jerking Lew from his thoughts. 'There are his boot tracks, and he headed that way and picked up his horse under those trees outside the yard when he heard me moving in on him. We should be able to get a good look at the prints of his horse, and if you can read that kind of thing then you might be able to catch him, even now.'

'I had plenty of experience tracking up in Montana,' Lew said, and checked the boot prints in the dust.

They reached the few trees growing outside the yard and came upon hoof prints. Lew bent to examine them,

51

but there was nothing in the way of distinguishing marks and he looked along the general direction of their departure to see if he could follow them.

'I'll head out now,' he mused. 'I need to come up with the rider, whoever he is. I reckon he could tell me a lot about what's been going on around here.'

'I'd like a shot at him myself,' Wishart said.

They went back to the corral and Lew caught his horse and saddled up. He led the animal over to the porch. Wishart looked around. He was carrying his Winchester, and was watching his surroundings.

'I'll bear in mind your invitation to stay here while I'm around,' Lew said, 'but I reckon I'll be too busy looking for badmen to rest up at all. I'll be happy if you can keep a tight rein on Wayne. He shouldn't be riding around loose any more, not until I've cleaned out the snakes.'

'Jane will keep him close to the ranch after this,' Wishart nodded. 'I hope you'll get lucky, Lew, but I got a feeling you'll need all the luck in the world to sort this out. Whoever's behind it has had several years to dig in.'

'At least there are men around who know exactly what is going on,' Lew replied. 'It will be a matter of finding one of them and making him talk about it.'

'That's easier said than done.' Wishart grimaced. 'Any time you need some help then let me know and I'll bring my crew on the hop. I got a bad feeling that what's happened to your father is gonna happen to me. Since I saw Abe Fenner at the bank I've noticed things going wrong around here.'

'I'll see Fenner when I can get around to him.' Lew looked around the yard. 'I have to start somewhere, and the bank is as good a place as any. My father took the money he got from the ranch out of Fenner's bank, and it disappeared along with Pa. See you around, Joe.'

'Keep in touch,' Wishart said.

Lew climbed into his saddle. He favoured his left leg as he rode out of the yard and followed the fence around to the trees where the intruder had tethered his horse. He checked the tracks again and then rode out, following the imprints of the hoofs, and soon came to the conclusion that the unknown man was heading towards Bostock. He rode steadily, watching the tracks intently, and kept an alert eye on his surroundings, only too aware that he had been shot at twice since returning to home range.

The sun burned down from a cloudless sky. Lew sweated as he continued. The range was humming with natural life. Cattle were grazing in the distance, and an air of peace surrounded him, but he realized it was an illusion. There was bad trouble on this range and his family was deeply involved. He wondered what had happened to his father, and thought endlessly about the possibilities, but he was no wiser by the time he sighted Bostock. The prints he was following headed straight to the rear of the livery barn. He reined in at the corral behind the barn and looked at the three horses inside it. Ed Faylen was standing in the open rear door of the stable, watching his approach, and came forward when Lew dismounted and tied his horse to the top rail of the corral.

'Looks like you found some more trouble,' Faylen said. 'You got blood all over the leg of your pants.'

'Do you mind if I check out those horses you got in the corral?' Lew countered.

'Go ahead. What are you looking for?'

'Are they your horses?'

'Sure! I rent them out occasionally.'

'Then take a look at these prints I've been following.' Lew pointed to the tracks in the dust. 'You should be familiar with the prints of your own horses. See if you can recognize them.'

Faylen squinted at the tracks. 'Say, they look like they were made by old Blackie,' he mused. 'Come and take a look at him.'

They entered the corral and Faylen picked up a rope halter from a post. He put it around the black's neck and retied it. When he lifted the animal's right foreleg he pointed to a nick in the horseshoe.

'That's all I need to see,' he said. 'You might not have noticed it in the tracks, but I did. Yeah, those tracks were made by Blackie. Where did you drop on to them?'

'Out at Box W. Who rented Blackie yesterday?'

Faylen scratched his head. 'Ossie Hanks picked him up around six for the evening. Said he was visiting a gal out of town. Blackie was back here when I checked this morning around six.'

'Who's Ossie Hanks?'

'He's Abe Fenner's bank guard and odd job man. What's he been up to? Is he the one that shot you in the leg? Did you trail Blackie all the way back to town?'

'I'd like to keep that quiet for now.' Lew looked into Faylen's dark eyes.

'I won't open my mouth about it,' Faylen replied stoutly. 'It ain't none of my business. But you wanta be careful around Hanks. He's a real tough man. That's why he's got that job at the bank. He was a detective in Kansas City before he came here. It wouldn't do to get on the wrong side of him.'

'I don't know him so he must be new around here. How long has he been in town?'

'A couple of years. Fenner knew him in Kansas City.'

'Thanks for the advice about him. I'll bear it in mind.' Lew nodded. 'Take care of my horse for me, huh? I've got some business at the bank this morning and I'll take a look at Hanks then, if he's around.'

'You look like you'd better see Doc Allen before you do anything else,' Faylen observed.

Lew sighed as he walked along the street to the doctor's house. Allen was in his office with a patient when Lew knocked at the front door, and Mrs Allen took him into a small waiting room. A few minutes later Doc Allen called him into the office.

'Someone has really got it in for you,' Allen commented.

Lew dropped his pants and stretched out on the examination couch.

'So what happened this time?' Allen asked as he examined the leg wound.

Lew explained tersely, and Allen stopped what he was doing when Ossie Hanks was mentioned.

'He is one bad man, Lew,' Allen warned. 'Watch your step around him.'

Lew told the doctor of Wayne's presence out at Box W. Allen shook his head.

'You're full of surprises this morning,' he mused. 'I'll drop in on Joe Wishart when I'm next out that way. I'd like to see what progress Wayne has made.'

'I'm certain now that my pa is dead, Doc,' Lew said tensely. 'He disappeared three years ago after leaving Kansas City to come back here to sort out his trouble, and he can't still be alive after that long a time.'

'You can't handle this situation alone, Lew,' Allen said firmly. 'You need to get the law in on this as soon as you can.'

'I wouldn't hesitate if Sheriff Parrish was still in the job, but I don't cotton to Shenton so I won't talk to him.'

'But you can't go around making your own investigation. If you happen to kill someone then you'll be booked for murder.'

'I'll take that chance. Someone is getting away with murder around here and I intend to find out who it is.'

Allen remained silent and treated Lew's wound. He could tell by Lew's manner that no amount of talking would change his mind, but he was worried. When he had bandaged the leg he clapped Lew on his uninjured shoulder.

'That's all I can do for you,' he said. 'Ideally, you should rest that leg for a few days, but I don't suppose you'll do that. Just be careful, Lew, and don't rush into this thing with your eyes closed. It'll only take one bullet to put you out of it permanently, and it seems there are some men around here who are playing for keeps. Who they are and what they're doing is not known at the moment, and they will do anything to keep it that way.'

'I know what the tally is, Doc.' Lew nodded. 'I've got a hand in this game whether I like it or not, and if my pa is dead then I'm gonna find the killer and make him pay for it.'

He left the doctor's house and stood looking around. The bank drew him immediately, and he crossed the street and paused at the entrance. He could see that there was very little business going on behind the big glass door, so entered, to be confronted immediately by a big man of around forty years old who looked as large as the side of a barn. He was wearing a dark blue town suit, a black string tie, and had three points of a folded handkerchief showing in the breast pocket of his jacket. He was hatless, and his fair hair was cropped so short it stuck up like bits of wire all over his skull. Lew thought he looked like a big ape dressed up in a suit. The man's dark eyes were expressionless, hard and unblinking, and his mouth was a thin-lipped slit under his bulbous nose.

'Good morning, sir.' The voice that issued from the mouth was low-pitched and, to Lew's ears, seemed filled with menace. 'I'm Ossie Hanks, the guard at this establishment. What is your business please?'

'I'm Lew Harper. I want to see Abe Fenner.'

Lew, watching Hanks' face intently, saw no reaction in the fleshy features, but a shadow seemed to brighten the brown eyes momentarily. It was gone in a flash but it warned Lew that his name was known to this man.

'I'll see if Mr Fenner is able to see you, sir,' Hanks said. 'I'll be only a minute.'

He turned away, walked to a door in the back wall, knocked politely, and entered, closing the door at his back. Lew gazed at the door, wondering what was being said inside the office, but Hanks had barely closed the door when it was opened again and Abe Fenner appeared in the doorway. The banker looked around quickly, saw

57

Lew, paused for a moment, and then advanced towards him with an outstretched hand, his smooth face creased in a welcoming smile.

'Lew Harper!' he declared in a welcoming tone. 'I'd heard you were back in town, and was hoping you would drop in to see me. How have you been, my boy? It's been at least five years, hasn't it? Come into my office and we'll chat. Ossie, I do not want to be disturbed for the next fifteen minutes.'

Fenner was a small man, neat and precise in his appearance and movements. His cheeks were clean-shaven. His blue eyes shone with friendliness. Lew had always liked the banker, but now he was suspicious of everyone in town, and would not let himself be misled by an affable manner. He followed Fenner into the office and sat down on a chair beside the big desk by the window overlooking the main street.

'I can see you've had some trouble since your return,' Fenner observed.

'I'm not the first one in my family to find trouble,' Lew replied. 'My brother Wayne was shot three years ago, and my pa has disappeared – at least, he hasn't been seen since he left for Kansas City. So the trouble has been around for a long time. I rode in yesterday and immediately walked into a gun trap. Then, last evening, I was at Box W when someone took a shot at me.'

'Have you any idea who's behind the shooting?' Fenner's face was expressionless, but his eyes were filled with question, and Lew sensed that he was hoping for a negative reply.

'I didn't know yesterday, but since then I've learned a

thing or two and I'll get down to checking out a few facts that might lead me to the troublemaker. That's why I wanted to see you, Mr Fenner. My pa left town three years ago with a considerable sum of money – the proceeds of the sale of Circle H. He took my brother to doctors in Kansas City and told them he was returning here to handle some trouble. But he was never seen again, not around here or in Kansas City, and I'm wondering if he was robbed and killed for his money.'

'He wasn't carrying a large sum of money, as I recall,' Fenner mused. 'When the sale of the ranch went through, he repaid the outstanding mortgage, and I gave him a banker's draft for a little over six thousand dollars, drawn against our associate bank in Kansas City. Joe Wishart saw me recently about your father's apparent disappearance and I checked with our branch in Kansas City. Your father deposited the banker's draft in an account there, and had it transferred back here when he left Kansas City, although he has not been in here to make a single withdrawal.'

'And the money is still here in his account?'

'Yes.' Fenner arose and went to a large filing cabinet in a corner, opened a drawer, and searched through it. He extracted a small card, brought it back to the desk, and handed it to Lew. 'Interest is calculated and added to the account annually,' he said.

Lew saw that a sum exceeding six thousand dollars had been credited to the account. He returned the card to the banker.

'So what has happened to your father?' Fenner mused. 'That is a mystery which must be solved. You should see the sheriff now and set wheels in motion. I should think there is very little you can do personally at this late stage.'

'I prefer to handle this myself,' Lew said resolutely, 'and I mean to get to the bottom of it.'

'I hope you'll succeed.' Fenner nodded. 'Have you any idea who could be at the back of the trouble?'

'No. But I'm hopeful I'll be able to jog someone's memory and learn something of what went on around here three years ago. There was even a mystery about why Jack Tate shot my brother Wayne, and I don't think the real reason will ever come out.'

'Have you seen Wayne? Can he throw any light on what happened?'

'I don't know where he is.' Lew shook his head, feeling disinclined to reveal his brother's whereabouts. 'I'll get around to finding him in time, but right now I wanta concentrate on the troublemakers.'

'If there is anything I can do to help then you have only to ask,' Fenner told him.

'Thanks, but I'll handle it myself.' Lew arose and made for the door, but paused and turned to face Fenner. 'How did you get a man like Hanks to act as your bank guard?'

Fenner seemed surprised by the sudden change of topic. 'Hanks was a good detective in Kansas City; recommended by the manager of our main bank there when Hanks decided to retire from the city police and head out this way. I have found him conscientious and reliable; he does the work of two men. He's a rare find, and I am very pleased with him.'

Lew felt a twinge in his left thigh as he departed. He found Hanks standing just outside the office and, as the man smiled, Lew told himself that very shortly he would

have a showdown with Hanks to find out why he had followed him out to the Box W ranch to shoot at him. He left
the bank feeling as if he had not asked the right questions
about the situation, and had a sneaking thought that if the
questions were right then he hadn't got the right answers.
The leading question in his own mind was if Fenner
himself was involved in the trouble.

He stood on the sidewalk outside the saloon and
looked around the street, considering his next move. He
did not want to talk to Shenton for obvious reasons, but
the matter was taken out of his hands when the sheriff
emerged from his office, saw him in front of the saloon,
and came quickly towards him.

'Say, what happened to you?' Shenton called when he
was within earshot. 'I looked for you last evening when I
got back but no one had seen you. Faylen, at the stable,
told me you had ridden out. So where did you go and what
happened?'

'Did you catch up with those two men?' Lew countered.

'No, I didn't. I trailed them as far as Dead Horse Creek
and lost their tracks on hard ground over that way.'

'Dead Horse Creek is on Circle H range. Did you check
out the ranch in case they stopped off there?'

'You don't have to tell me my job,' Shenton said force-
fully. 'Of course I went there. I needed to talk to Cleaver
Nolan, to hear his side of what happened between you
two. His facts coincided fairly well with yours, but he said
he was only doing his job and you went over the top to get
him to talk. He wanted to make a charge of assault against
you but I talked him out of it. You'd better be careful after
this. You said you were a deputy sheriff in Montana; well,

that don't cut no ice around here, so pull in your horns and let me handle this business. That's what I get paid for. I can understand your feelings, but you can't go around taking the law into your own hands. That way, you'll either get shot or I'll have to come down on you for infringing the law.'

'I know enough about the law to understand that I can defend myself,' Lew said. 'If you wanta bring the law in on this then I've got something for you to investigate. I was shot out at Box W last evening, and stayed there during the night. This morning I followed hoof prints in from the ranch, where Joe Wishart saw an intruder, and found the horse that left the tracks in the corral, back of the livery barn. Faylen identified the prints and said the horse was rented out for the evening to Ossie Hanks, who said he wanted to visit a girl living out of town. It seems an open and shut case to me. I saw Hanks at the bank this morning when I went in to talk to Fenner, and I reckon he has some awkward questions to answer.'

'Did you say anything to him about what happened last evening?' Shenton asked.

'No. I decided to leave it to you.'

'I'll go along there now and have a word with him.' Shenton hitched up his gun-belt and turned away, then swung back to face Lew. 'What did you see Fenner about?' he demanded.

'Financial business, that's all.'

Shenton nodded and went on along the boardwalk to the bank. Lew remained motionless and watched the sheriff until he entered the bank, then turned and went back to the livery barn. He planned to ride out on the trail of the two men who had set up the gun trap the day before and try to find them.

Ed Faylen was forking hay into his loft from a wagon that had just pulled into town. The livery man jumped to the ground when he saw Lew.

'Did you tackle Hanks about last night?' Faylen demanded.

Lew shook his head. 'I've turned that business over to the sheriff,' he replied. 'It's his job. If I confronted Hanks, it would likely end in shooting.'

'Now you're showing sense. No one in his right mind would willingly go up against Hanks. He carries two guns, one stuck in his belt in the small of his back and the other in a shoulder holster. He's real fast with each of them. I've seen him practising out by my corral of a Sunday morning. What are you gonna do now?'

'Just take a ride, that's all.' Lew had no intention of talking about his future movements.

He saddled up and led the horse out back, where he tied the animal to the corral, then slipped back into the barn when Faylen went up to the loft. He approached Shenton's horse, which was standing in a stall just inside the front door, and checked the animal's hoofs, wanting to be able to identify its tracks out on the range. Then he rode out, and found it a simple matter to follow the sheriff's route of the previous afternoon.

He saw that Shenton had followed the two sets of prints left by the ambushers, but his expression changed when he reached the spot where Shenton had confronted the men. The prints left a clear picture of what had taken place. Shenton had halted and so had the ambushers, and they had remained together for some minutes, which was obvious from the muddle of prints where the three animals had moved restlessly on short reins. Then the two unknown gunnies had ridden off in the direction of Circle H while the sheriff hed headed north in the direction of Dead Horse Creek.

Lew sat his saddle, massaging his throbbing thigh while reading the tangled signs. He decided to check on the sheriff before resuming his search for the ambushers, and set off on the trail of the single set of prints. He sent the horse on at a fast pace, and came eventually to Dead Horse Creek, shimmering in the bright sunlight. Shenton had let his horse drink before angling south-west to ride into Circle H as he had reported, but he had lied about losing the tracks of the two gunnies. He had confronted them, let them go free, and Lew was keen to find out why.

He kept under cover when he sighted the ranch, dismounted, and left his horse tied to a bush in a small copse, a hundred yards out from the front yard. He drew his Winchester and moved forward to get closer, hunkering down behind a stack of logs beside the barn to relax while looking around. There were four horses in the corral.

Lew went on to the side of the house and flattened himself against the left front corner. There were no signs of life, and he wondered what Nolan was doing. Silence pressed in around him, and he began to think he was the only man in this part of the world, until he heard the sound of approaching hoofs and saw a rider approaching from the west. Lew eased back from the corner and removed his Stetson in order to peer out at the newcomer.

The rider, mounted on a good-looking dun, entered

the yard and rode leisurely towards the porch. He uttered a rebel yell that echoed around the yard as he reined in and dismounted. Lew eased forward a fraction to get a better look, but the man's hat brim shielded his features as he stood waiting by the head of his horse. A moment later Lew heard the front door of the house creak open and Cleaver Nolan appeared. Nolan was grinning.

'Hey, Jack,' Nolan called. 'Come and have a drink to celebrate your return.'

The man called Jack swept off his hat and waved it in the air as he uttered another rebel yell. Lew stared at the upturned face and a cold pang darted through him. He knew Jack's second name without being told: it was Jack Tate, who had shot Wayne three years before and was supposed to be securely locked behind bars.

# FIVE

Lew stared in disbelief at Tate. The man was supposed to be in prison. So what was he doing here? Had he been released? Lew doubted that. He recalled Doc Allen saying that Tate had made an unsuccessful escape bid and received an extra two years in jail for his efforts. At that moment Tate's raucous voice cut through Lew's thoughts, and an echoing peal of laughter rang across the yard.

'The hell they turned me loose!' Tate yelled in reply to a question from Nolan. 'Me and two pards busted out! We killed a guard and made a run for it, and this time they couldn't stop us. So I'm back and ready to make things hum around here again. All I wanta know, Nolan, is where the Harpers are. I wanta finish that job I started on Wayne Harper, and then I'll take care of the rest of his brood.'

Lew tensed as he listened, and reached for his pistol, but Tate's next words stopped him and he remained in concealment.

'My two pards are lying low back the rise over there. I reckoned to come on in and see if it's safe for us to show our faces.'

'Yeah, you'll be OK,' Nolan replied. 'Get your pards and come on in. You'll be safe here, like a bug in a rug.'

Hoofs pounded the yard and Lew peered out to see Tate riding back to the gate. He watched the hardcase head for the nearest rise, waving his hat over his head in a come-on signal, and presently two riders appeared and came at a gallop towards the ranch. They hammered across the yard and headed for the corral. Lew leaned back against the wall of the house to consider this development. He fought against an impulse to draw his gun and confront the hardcases, and after some consideration decided to withdraw. Tate's arrival on the scene changed the situation drastically, and from what he had overheard, Lew's suspicions of a crooked deal being worked were substantiated.

He eased away from the house and sought cover outside the yard, then began to work his way around to the spot where he had left his horse, fighting the urge to take up the challenge made by Tate's arrival. He passed the small fenced-in area that contained the grave of his mother, and the sight of it set his impulses flaring again. The very presence of those hardmen in the ranch house was pure sacrilege, and he fought against the impulse to turn around and head for a showdown, but common sense prevailed, for to give way to his feelings would bring the crooked Buck Shenton on his trail with all the weight and power of the law behind him. There had to be another way of handling it – one that would not claim his own life in the process.

He entered the thicket and his horse whickered softly. Lew halted and looked around. A faint movement to his left caught his attention, and he froze when he saw a man rising up out of the undergrowth with a levelled pistol in his hand. He immediately lifted his hands clear of his waist.

'So, who are you and what are you doing here?' the man demanded. 'How come you're sneaking around this place like a thief in the night?'

'Who are you?' Lew countered.

'I've got the gun so I'll ask the questions,' the man grinned. 'But you sneaking around here points to you being unfriendly to Cleaver Nolan and the riff-raff that just rode in.'

'You can say that again,' Lew replied. 'And you hiding out here puts you against Nolan. I'm Lew Harper. This spread belonged to my father.'

'Joe told me about you. I'm Pete Elrington. I ride for Joe Wishart. Me and my two pards crew the Box W. We got back from Buffalo Crossing this morning with some new stock, and Joe sent me here to keep an eye on this place – sort of watch the comings and goings and make a note of the details.'

Lew heaved a sigh. 'Did you recognize any of the riders who rode into the ranch?'

'No. They're strangers to me.' Elrington was not much older than Lew; thick-set and with an easy smile. His brown eyes were steady. Lew liked him instinctively.

'One of them is Jack Tate, who shot my brother Wayne three years ago and went to prison for it. I reckon he's busted out of jail, and he's back here to cause more trouble.'

'What do you wanta do about them? If you like, I'll

hang around here and watch them while you go for the sheriff.'

'That's out. I think Shenton is crooked.' Lew gave an account of his actions since his arrival, and Elrington shook his head.

'I never did cotton to Shenton,' he mused. 'There's something about him I don't like. But him being on the opposite side of the fence makes life a lot harder for you, huh? How are you gonna handle this? I'll go along with anything you wanta do.'

'I reckon there are too many for me to go up against. I got it figured that there are maybe six men in the house. If Tate and his pair of sidewinders hadn't showed up I would have gone in after Nolan and the two men who ambushed me in town yesterday, but now the odds are too great. Instead of going for them bald-headed, I'll have to try a different approach. I need to get some evidence against Shenton, and maybe Casey Mitchell in town. But how I'll manage that I don't rightly know at the moment.'

'Someone's coming,' Elrington warned in a sharp undertone.

Lew frowned, hearing nothing, but a moment later he caught the sound of hoofs coming from the direction of Bostock. He drew his gun and moved to the edge of the copse. He saw a rider approaching; surprise hit him when he recognized Ossie Hanks.

'Well I'll be damned!' he exclaimed. 'Look what the wind's blowing in. This feller shot me in the leg last night out at Box W; leastways, he rode the horse the gunnie used, and I'm sure he was riding that animal.'

'The hell you say!' Elrington jerked his pistol from its

holster. 'Let's grab the buzzard and clip his wings.'

Lew reached out a hand to restrain Elrington as Hanks came to the outer edge of the trees and skirted them. They crouched in the undergrowth until the bank guard had gone on towards the ranch.

'Why didn't you grab him?' Elrington demanded when Hanks was out of earshot.

'I can't do a thing about him or any of them until I have proof of their wrongdoing,' Lew replied. 'They've got a crooked sheriff in their back pocket, and that's the rub.'

'Yeah, he does tie your hands.' Elrington shook his head. 'You sure got the dirty end of the stick.'

'And then some,' Lew added.

'They watched Hanks ride into the ranch and pull up at the porch. Nolan appeared in the doorway of the house and greeted Hanks like a long-lost brother. Lew wished he was close enough to hear the conversation that passed between them. But the bank guard did not dismount and, whatever he said, Nolan's action was surprising. The big man turned abruptly and dashed into the house. A moment later, he reappeared in the doorway, smiling broadly. Lew frowned as he tried to make sense of the by-play. Elrington moved uneasily.

'What was that all about?' Elrington demanded. 'Who else is in the house? Nolan has passed a message to them.'

'Jack Tate and his two pards, and probably the two men who set the gun trap in town yesterday.'

'Why would a man from the bank ride out here with a message?' Elrington persisted.

'I wish I knew,' Lew replied.

They waited in silence, watching Nolan and Hanks

talking. The sun was beating down relentlessly and the heat had become intolerable. Then, with shocking suddenness, three riders appeared from the rear of the house and came across the yard at a gallop. They raised dust as they swung in the direction of the copse where Lew and Elrington were concealed.

'They're wise to us,' Lew observed. 'Hanks must have spotted us in passing. We should get outa here.'

'Too late,' Elrington replied. 'They're too close. They'll have us cold out in the open.'

Lew watched the oncoming riders. Jack Tate was leading them, and the trio had pistols in their hands. He saw the sense in Elrington's words and drew his gun. He had wanted to avoid contact with the badmen because the law was on their side, but Jack Tate was an escaped prisoner, and that was a horse of a different colour.

'The leading rider is Jack Tate,' he told Elrington. 'He's supposed to be in prison for several more years so I suspect he's escaped, and the law will certainly want him back. Let's see if we can take him alive, huh?'

Elrington lifted his gun and cocked it. The next instant the three riders cut loose with their weapons and gunfire rattled and echoed. Lew heard bullets crackling and thudding into the trees. He dropped to one knee and prepared to fight. At last he was facing his enemies on something like equal terms.

Jack Tate emptied his pistol in a blast of fire. Lew ducked the slugs and drew a bead on the man. He fired, and gunsmoke blew back into his face. He saw Tate jerk under the impact of the slug before pitching out of his saddle. The other two riders came on without hesitation,

71

shooting rapidly, and Elrington downed one with his first shot. The third man veered away and disappeared around the side of the copse. Elrington ran through the sparse trees to the opposite side, shooting at the rider as he disappeared over a crest to the rear.

Lew looked at the ranch yard. Nolan was still standing in the doorway of the house but Hanks and his horse were no longer in view. Lew returned his attention to Tate, who was stretched out in the dust. The other hardcase was huddled on the ground a few yards to Tate's left. Lew cocked his gun and left the cover of the trees to cross to where Tate was lying. He saw Tate's gun on the ground nearby and bent over the man, expecting to find him dead, but Tate, although unconscious, had a bloodstain on the right side of his chest and was still breathing. Lew checked the second man, and found him dead.

He glanced at the ranch house again, saw that Nolan was no longer in view, and looked around for Tate's mount. The animal was grazing several yards away. Elrington came back to Lew.

'What do we do now?' he demanded.

'Tate is still alive.' Lew had already decided on his next move. 'I'm gonna haul him into town and toss him into Shenton's lap to see which way the sheriff will jump. I'm gonna change my tactics after this. I won't make any headway just by riding around watching these men. I've got to get proof of what they're doing. There's Fenner at the bank and Mitchell in the saloon, and they seem to be bossing whatever is going on. I need to get close to them. But whoever is back of this trouble, they're dug in deep.'

'Let's get Tate across his horse,' Elrington said. 'I'll ride into town with you. I'll tell Wishart I'm wasting my time out here just watching. I don't know how you're going to get at the roots of this business, but I'm with you all the way, Lew. Wishart told me to stick with you when you showed up, and I'll do just that.'

'Don't stick too close to me,' Lew said. 'It could turn out to be dangerous.'

Tate's chest injury did not seem to be much more than a flesh wound, and he was regaining his senses when he was put face downward across his saddle and roped into place. Elrington led the horse as they set out for Bostock, and Lew dropped back to watch the ranch for movement until Elrington had a good start. There was no movement on the ranch, but Lew did not doubt that a sharp watch was being kept by Nolan. He rode out to catch up with Elrington, and they continued along the trail to town.

Lew wondered what had become of Hanks, and watched his surroundings as they rode. They reached Bostock without incident, and paused at the end of the main street.

'It looks quiet,' Elrington observed.

'Too quiet,' Lew replied. 'You don't have to ride in with me. Stay out here while I see what kind of a reception I get.

'I don't see what Shenton can do against you. Tate was shot in self-defence. He and his two pards were trying to kill you. Heck, they threw enough lead at us to kill a troop of US cavalry. And as I was on the receiving end of it I'll go right along with you to back you up.'

Lew nodded. 'Then you'd better keep your eyes open and your hand on your gun,' he warned.

They rode to the law office and dismounted. Lew untied Tate, dragged him off the horse and stretched him out on the sidewalk.

'I'll fetch Doc Allen,' Elrington said, and rode off along the street.

Lew entered the law office. Buck Shenton was seated behind his desk, and he shot to his feet when he looked up and recognized Lew.

'Say, where did you get to?' Shenton demanded. 'I've been looking all over for you. I spoke to Ossie Hanks after you told me what you thought happened last night, and he told me he didn't leave town. He was going to but changed his mind at the last moment when he heard about a poker game in the back room of the saloon.'

'So what about the horse he rented?'

'He didn't use it. Someone else must have taken it and followed you out to Box W.'

'And you'll take Hanks' word for that, huh?'

'The hell I did! I checked him out, and he's got an alibi for the whole of yesterday evening, right up till one o'clock in the morning, I spoke to the other poker players, and they all bear out his statement. Too many witnesses saw Hanks in the saloon for it to be a lie, and why would anyone want to lie on his behalf?'

'Did you talk to Ed Faylen? He said Hanks went out on the horse.'

'I got his story, and he didn't actually see Hanks ride out. Hanks rented the horse, but he didn't ride it, so I'm afraid there's nothing I can do about him, Harper. You're flogging a dead horse with Hanks.' He grinned as if he had made a joke.

74

'It's obviously a set-up,' Lew said.

'I wouldn't know.' Shenton shook his head. 'According to the law you haven't got a leg to stand on. It's open and shut against you.'

'OK.' Lew nodded. 'So tell me about Jack Tate.'

'Tate?' Shenton frowned. 'Where the hell does he come into it?'

'He's supposed to be in jail, ain't he?'

'Not any longer. I got a wire from the state capital last evening warning me to be on the watch for Tate. He broke jail five days ago – him and two others. I'm gonna get some Wanted posters printed and distributed when I can get around to it.'

'You don't have to. He's lying on the boardwalk outside with a bullet in his chest. He attacked me out at Circle H earlier this morning, and I nailed him.'

Shenton was shocked. A change of expression flashed across his face as he digested the information. His jaw dropped and he stared at Lew for a moment, his eyes widening. Then he gulped and hurried to the street door and peered out. Lew followed him and saw Shenton drop to one knee beside Tate to examine him closely. At that moment Doc Allen came across the street, carrying his medical bag, and Pete Elrington rode up and dismounted.

Doc Allen looked inquiringly at Lew but said nothing, and Lew remained silent. They watched the doctor examine Tate, who was barely conscious, and Allen nodded as he regained his feet.

'The three of us should manage him,' Shenton said, and Lew nodded.

They picked up Tate, carried him across the street to

Doc Allen's office, and placed him on a couch. Lew headed for the street again immediately, followed closely by Elrington. Shenton called to Lew.

'Don't leave town until I've had a chance to get a statement from you,' he directed.

'I'll stick around too,' Elrington said. 'I was with Harper when Tate and those other two attacked us without warning.'

Shenton grimaced and looked Elrington up and down. He shook his head. 'What happened to the two men who were with Tate?' he demanded.

'One's lying dead by the Circle H yard,' Elrington replied. 'I killed him. The third one rode over a ridge and got away.'

Shenton nodded and returned to Doc Allen and Tate. Lew and Elrington went on across the street, untied their mounts, and rode to the livery barn. As they entered, Lew heard a commotion coming from the stable office – a voice shouting. He went across and saw Ossie Hanks manhandling Faylen. The big bank guard was slapping Faylen's face with heavy right-handers, and the livery man was sagging in his grasp. Lew drew his pistol and slammed it against Hanks' head. Hanks' hat saved him from the worst of the blow, but he dropped to his knees as if he had been poleaxed. Faylen leaned against a wall. Blood was running from a cut over his left eye. He staggered to his desk and dropped into the chair.

Elrington drew his pistol and stood over Hanks. Lew bent over Faylen.

'Are you all right?' he asked. 'What started this?'

Faylen looked up. He wiped blood from his face and

looked at his fingers. His face was pale beneath its tan, and he was shaking.

'He just rode in from out of town, and attacked me for no reason at all,' Faylen said hesitantly. 'It was to do with renting that horse last night. He said if I spoke to anyone else about it he'd kill me. I don't believe he was playing poker last night. I'm sure he rode the horse out of town.'

'There's enough evidence now to have Hanks put behind bars,' Lew said. 'All you'll have to do is swear out a complaint against him.'

'And who'll protect me from him and his friends?' Faylen demanded. 'I don't have a chance against the likes of them.'

'If I can prove he shot me last night they'll put him away for a long time,' Lew said. 'We'll take him along to the law office and hear what Shenton has to say about it.'

Elrington stuck the muzzle of his pistol under Hanks' nose. The big man was shaking his head. His eyes were open but he seemed dazed.

'Get up,' Elrington commanded. 'You're going to jail.'

Lew remained in the background, gun ready. He watched Hanks struggle to his feet. Elrington moved in close and removed the pistol from Hanks' shoulder holster. Hanks staggered forward a couple of steps, still shaking his head. He reached behind his back with his right hand, and, the next instant, had produced the gun he carried in the waistband.

Hanks fired at Elrington. The blasting crash of the shot rocked the small office and bits of straw floated down from the loft. As Elrington fell to his knees, Hanks jerked his gun around to cover Lew, but Lew was already moving forward. He slammed the long barrel of his pistol against the wrist of Hanks' gun hand and the weapon fell to the ground. Lew followed up with a back-handed swipe to Hank's left temple, and the impact sent Hanks off balance. He fell against the desk and rolled to the floor.

Lew bent over Hanks, saw he was unconscious, and kicked away his discarded gun. He straightened and looked at Faylen behind the desk. The livery man's face was frozen in a grimace of fear. Lew turned to Elrington, who was lying motionless, face-down, and was shocked to find the cowboy dead, with blood dribbling from the centre of his chest and saturating the fabric of his shirt.

The echoes of the shot faded slowly. Lew struggled to maintain his composure as he turned his attention to a badly shaken Faylen.

'Did you see what happened here, Faylen?' he demanded.

'I sure did!' Faylen's voice sounded hollow. 'It was sudden death. I never saw anything like it. Hanks shot your pard in cold blood, and you knocked him senseless before he could shoot you.' He shook his head. 'Sudden death,' he repeated, as if trying to come to terms with the fact.

'Sit there until Shenton arrives,' Lew said. 'Then tell him exactly how it happened.' He picked up Hanks' pistol and tossed it on the desk in front of Faylen. 'Use that to keep Hanks quiet if he comes to before I get back, and shoot him if you have to.'

'You can't leave me here alone with Hanks,' Faylen gasped. 'He'll kill me!'

'Not while you've got his gun,' Lew rasped. 'Go on, pick

it up. Keep him covered. I won't be long. The sound of the shot should bring Shenton on the run.'

Faylen picked up the pistol; his hand shook so badly he had to rest his elbows on the desk top and hold the weapon in both hands. Lew waited a moment for the livery man to regain his composure before leaving the office. He was badly shocked by the death of Pete Elrington, but satisfaction filled him when he considered the situation in which Ossie Hanks would find himself when he came to his senses.

Townsmen were already converging on the livery barn from all over town, and Lew saw Buck Shenton coming at a half-run from the doctor's house. He holstered his gun and leaned against the door of the barn, hoping that at last he was making some headway in this shady business. He was optimistic as he awaited the arrival of the crooked sheriff.

# SIX

Shenton was sweating when he reached Lew. He pushed through the gathering crowd of men, ignoring the shouted questions about the shooting. Lew turned to re-enter the barn as the sheriff paused to regain his breath.

'In here, Sheriff,' Lew said sharply, moving to the door of Faylen's office.

He stopped in the doorway and permitted the lawman to enter first. Shenton stepped into the office and paused.

'Jeez!' He gasped as he took in the grim scene. 'What in hell happened here?' He turned to face Lew with accusation lining in his face.

'Talk to Faylen,' Lew said. 'He saw everything.'

Faylen, gripping the pistol and covering Hanks, who had regained his senses, began gabbling incoherently, and Shenton went to the desk and slammed his hand upon it.

'Whoa up there, Faylen!' he rapped. 'Calm down. Take a deep breath, count to ten, and then talk.'

Lew listened to Faylen's account of the incident; the livery man told it exactly as it had occurred. Shenton glanced at Lew from time to time but did not interrupt the narrative. When Faylen lapsed into silence, Shenton considered for a moment, and then cleared his throat.

'Are you sure that is exactly what happened?' he demanded.

Faylen nodded emphatically. 'I swear to it, as God is my witness,' he gasped. He jerked open a drawer in his desk, produced a half-empty bottle of whiskey, and swigged from it.

'You got anything to add to Faylen's statement?' Shenton asked Lew. 'I suppose you were in the thick of it.'

'All the way,' Lew agreed. 'You've got the rights of it, and Faylen has told the truth.'

'OK.' Shenton toed Hanks. 'Get on your feet, Hanks. You know where the jail is. Faylen, drop by my office later and I'll get your statement in writing.' He glanced at Lew. 'I'll need a statement from you about what you saw. What are you gonna do now?'

'I'll ride out to Box W and tell Joe Wishart about Pete Elrington,' Lew replied.

'What was Elrington doing at Circle H earlier?'

'As far as I know, he was just riding by.'

Shenton shook his head as if he did not believe Lew. 'You'd better watch your step in future,' he growled.

Lew fetched his horse, which had wandered into an empty stall when he'd dropped its reins before going to the stable office. He led it outside and swung into the saddle. Shenton emerged from the barn just behind him to take Hanks to the law office. Lew stood watching them until they went inside. He felt uneasy about the situation, and was thoughtful as he set out for Box W. He felt bad about the death of Pete Elrington although he had known the cowboy for only a couple of hours, and mentally added another debt to the account of the unknown men behind the trouble.

Shenton walked behind Hanks as they moved along the boardwalk to the law office. When they were out of earshot from Lew, Hanks half-turned his head and glanced at Shenton. He opened his mouth to start talking and Shenton snarled at him like a mad dog.

'Stow it until we get into the office,' he rapped. 'Keep going, and try to look as if you're under arrest.'

'You can't arrest me,' Hanks said stolidly.

'Try telling me something I don't know.' Shenton glanced over his shoulder and saw Lew riding along the street on his way out of town. 'You've made a real mess of things since last night. Now shut your mouth before I lose my temper and shut it for you. You've made all the wrong moves since Lew Harper came to town.'

They entered the law office and Shenton relaxed. He motioned to the chair beside the desk and Hanks dropped into it with a sigh of relief. A trickle of blood had dried on Hank's forehead and he probed the area with his thick fingers.

'So what the hell happened?' Shenton demanded.

'You might well ask.' Hanks growled in his throat like an angry bear. 'I had to go out to Circle H to leave some papers, and what do you think I found when I got there?' He paused as if expecting a response from Shenton but the sheriff merely gazed at him. 'I spotted Harper and a cowboy hiding in a stand of trees by the ranch yard, and Nolan was in the ranch house with Tate and the other two escaped prisoners, acting like they didn't have a care in the world. God knows what would have happened if I hadn't showed up. I told Nolan he was being watched and he sent Tate and the others out to deal with Harper. Tate got himself shot and one of the others was killed. The third man escaped and disappeared over the nearest ridge. I made myself scarce and came back to town at a gallop.'

'So what happened in the livery barn?' Shenton demanded.

'I confronted Faylen when I rode in. He must have talked to Harper. He certainly told Harper about me renting that horse last night. Fenner told me to kill Harper out on the range, but Harper got lucky. Now he's hit us. I was warning Faylen to keep his mouth shut when Harper walked in on me. I had to do something, and Elrington, not Harper, collected a slug.'

'So what do we do now?' Shenton asked.

Hanks shrugged. 'As I see it, Faylen and Harper have got to die. With them out of the way there'll be no witnesses to what happened.'

'You just might be able to handle Faylen,' Shenton observed, 'but Harper is another matter. You couldn't kill him out at Box W, and now I guess you'll never be able to.'

'Then you get after him and do the job,' Hanks snarled. 'Ain't that what you get paid for?'

'I'll take care of him when the time is right.' Shenton grimaced. 'In the meantime you're gonna have to sit in jail to make the situation look right. I can't have a killer wandering around town. What would folks say?'

'See Fenner and tell him what's happened.' Hanks said angrily. 'He won't be happy with me behind bars.'

'Let's find out how happy you'll be.' Shenton picked up a bunch of cell keys and motioned for Hanks to precede him into the cell block beyond the office. Hanks entered a cell and sat down to test the hardness of the bunk. He looked up as Shenton locked the door.

'See Fenner real soon,' he rasped. 'I've got better things to do than sit around here all day.'

Shenton went back into the office and sat at his desk to think things over, but it was already obvious to him that Lew Harper had to be put down, and the sooner the better. He left the office, locked the street door at his back, and went along to the bank. He walked into Fenner's office without knocking, and startled the banker, who was looking at a pile of accounts.

'Why the devil don't you knock?' Fenner demanded irritably.

'You've got big trouble.' Shenton sat on a corner of Fenner's desk. He gave an account of what he had learned of the trouble out at Circle H, and topped it up with a description of what he had seen in the office at the livery barn. 'So I had no option but to put Hanks behind bars,' he said, keeping his tone free from satisfaction. 'You've always set great store by Hanks, but I've never liked him. He ain't cut out for this sort of thing, and I don't trust him, anyway. He's made a mess of warning Faylen off, and I've got to go out now and put matters right. The only way I can do that is by killing Harper, which won't look good in view of what happened to the rest of his family. Folks will start putting two and two together, and might come up with the truth.'

'We'll have to take that chance,' Fenner mused. 'You'd

better keep Hanks behind bars for a few days. We have another two ranches to buy up before we can relax. When we've got them in hand we can sit back and wait for events to catch up with us. But what we don't need at this time is a scandal of any kind, so take care of Harper, and make it permanent. Let him vanish like his father did. With him gone, all links with that part of the business will be severed.'

'There's still Wayne Harper around somewhere.'

'He's not in his right mind, and will probably never remember what happened.'

'OK.' Shenton shrugged. 'If you're happy with that then I'm not going to worry about it. But I know that I wouldn't take any chances at all in such a high-stake game. And there's another matter that needs attention. Ed Faylen talked to Harper about Hanks, and he witnessed Hanks shooting Elrington. We don't need him around to talk about what he saw. So what do you want me to do about him?'

'You take care of it, but don't shoot him.' Fenner waved a dismissive hand. 'Crack his head and leave him lying in a stall in the barn with one of his wilder horses. It'll look like an accident. And then there's Jack Tate. It cost us a lot of money to have him sprung out of jail, and the first thing he's done is spoil his chances. Now everyone will know he's back in circulation, and I wanted to keep him up my sleeve for special jobs. Joe Wishart is being difficult about selling up so we've got to put more pressure on him. I was going to use Tate to kidnap the Wishart girl and hold her until Wishart comes round to our way of thinking.'

'I'll put Tate behind bars when Doc Allen has finished

with him, but I won't inform the authorities that I've got him. I'll sneak him out of town one dark night and turn him loose. He might do some good by killing Wishart, which will leave Jane Wishart in control, and she'll be much easier to handle than her father. I reckon you'll have a lot of trouble with Joe Wishart if he's not dealt with. He won't be a pushover.'

'In view of what happened at Circle H with the Harpers, I guess it might be better to kill Wishart out of hand. If you're going to kill Lew Harper then take Wishart out also. Then we'll see how that affects our business.'

'OK. You've only got to say what you want and it'll be done.' Shenton got up from the desk and walked to the door.

'I'll leave it to you to do what you think is necessary,' Fenner called after him.

Shenton shrugged as he went along the street to the livery barn. He didn't like the way the situation was panning out, but he was ready for any setback, and if the situation worsened he could cut his losses and head for other parts before the rot set in. He saddled up, led his horse out the back door, and tethered it behind the grain barn at the rear. He looked around to check that he wasn't being observed before stealing back into the stable with murder in mind. . . .

As Lew rode the trail to the Box W he began to get the feeling that he was being followed. At first it was just an involuntary shiver along his spine; an impulse to check his back trail more often, and when he saw nothing suspicious his uneasiness increased, for his senses never failed him. Three years as a deputy sheriff in Montana had honed his instincts to an extra degree of sharpness, and when he tried to ignore the feeling it developed into a certainty and began to enlarge in his mind until he finally found a suitable spot to conceal his horse. Then dropped into cover to watch his surroundings.

He threw himself down in a depression where several bushes were growing. His horse began grazing on the reverse side of a ridge behind him, and he kept a sharp watch on his back trail. He was not surprised when a lone rider suddenly appeared slightly off to the left of his trail, obviously following his tracks. Lew drew his pistol and checked its loads. He waited patiently until the man was almost within an arm's length before lunging to his feet and covering him with the weapon.

Lew recognized the man as the hardcase that had fled the shooting, which had claimed Tate and one of his pards at Circle H. The man's horse shied at Lew's unexpected appearance, and the rider had to struggle to bring the animal back under control.

'Say, what's going on?' he demanded when he finally settled his mount. 'Where the hell did you come from?'

'Don't act innocent with me,' Lew told him. 'I saw you a couple of hours ago charging at me at Circle H when Tate and your other pard was shot. I don't know your name but I know you escaped from prison five days ago. So why are you following me? I reckon you were thinking of bushwhacking me.'

'I reckon you've got me mixed up with someone else,' the man replied. 'I'm Harvey Tulse. I heard in town that Box W might want an extra rider so I'm heading out that way.'

'I got a good look at you at Circle H,' Lew responded, 'and I've got you dead to rights, Tulse, if that is your name. Just keep your hands away from your gun. I'm hair-triggered, and I'm getting a mite tired of being shot at. I'll take you with me to Box W, and haul you to jail in Bostock afterwards. The sheriff will discover who you are. Now get rid of your weapons.'

With Lew's gun pointing steadily at his chest, Tulse, a tall, lean man of thirty, with a hard face and cruel eyes, had no option but to disarm himself. Lew left the weapons lying in the grass and motioned for Tulse to ride ahead. They continued to Box W. Joe Wishart emerged from the house when Lew entered the yard. Wishart was carrying his Winchester, and lifted its muzzle to cover Tulse when he noticed that Tulse was unarmed and Lew was holding his pistol.

'Who have you got there, Lew?' Wishart called.

'Harvey Tulse. He crashed out of prison a few days ago with Jack Tate. I'm afraid I've got some bad news for you, Joe.'

Wishart's craggy face changed expression and he grimaced. 'Bad news is all I get these days,' he said. 'What's wrong?'

Lew gave details of the shooting at Circle H, and rounded off with a terse account of the trouble in the livery barn in town. Wishart clenched his teeth at the news of Elrington's death. He heaved a sigh and shook his head sorrowfully.

'Jane will be mighty sad to hear about this,' he said. He glanced at Tulse. 'How was he involved?'

Lew shrugged. 'I caught him trailing me from town; no

doubt planning to bushwhack me.'

'Maybe we can get him to talk.' Wishart cocked his rifle and aimed at Tulse's chest. 'What have you got to say, mister?' he demanded.

Tulse looked down the barrel of the long gun, saw Wishart's shocked face behind the weapon, and gained the impression that his last moment had come. He held up both hands as if to ward off the inevitable shot.

'Don't be hasty, mister,' he said. 'I only hit this range this morning. I'm a stranger from nowhere, and I don't know what's going on around here. Jack Tate is the local man, and when we busted out of prison he said we'd be OK if we made it to this place. But all hell broke loose before we had time to relax at that ranch. I took out when the shooting started, and that's all I can tell you.'

'You know a lot more than that,' Lew said harshly. 'If it was as you said then you would have kept going when Tate was shot out of his saddle. But you didn't run. Instead, you rode to town, and followed my trail when I came on here, so you've got to know more than you're letting on. You're standing on the edge right now, looking into hell, and if you've got any sense you'll start talking, because if you don't, by sunset you'll be lying under this range with six feet of earth on your chest.'

'If I knew anything I'd tell you,' Tulse said desperately. 'I don't know anyone around here.'

'I'll turn him over to my other two riders,' Wishart suggested. 'Elrington was a good pard of theirs, and they'd welcome the chance of dealing with someone connected with the men causing trouble on this range. Go on in the house, Lew, and talk to Jane. Tell her what's happened. I'll

89

come back to you when this feller has opened his trap.'

Lew nodded and stepped on to the porch. He paused to look around the yard, and saw two cowpunchers working over by the corral. Wishart called to them and they came across the yard.

'Appleton and Davis,' Wishart introduced. 'Meet Lew Harper, boys. He's gonna put an end to the trouble around here.'

'I wish I had your confidence,' Lew observed.

He shook hands with the two punchers and turned to enter the house, reluctant to spread the bad news he carried. He was dubious about joining forces with anyone. All he needed was to learn what had happened to his father, and he was determined not to rest until he had wormed the information out of someone who possessed the facts.

Jane was busy in the kitchen when Lew entered the house, and she listened impassively as he narrated the incidents he had experienced. When he told her about Elrington's death she uttered a gasp and her face turned deathly pale. Lew grasped her arm and led her to a chair.

'Poor Pete,' she said in a low tone. 'He was such a nice man. He deserved better than that. What's going on around here, Lew? What are these troublemakers after? It seems as if they're grabbing range, but I'm sure there's more to it than that. A man called on Pa last week offering to buy the ranch for a ridiculously low sum, and Pa practically threw him out on his ear. And that's how it started with your father, I seem to recall. He rode over here about three years ago and said he'd been offered money to sell up. It was when he refused the deal that his troubles started.'

'This is the first I've heard about it,' Lew said. 'Have you any idea who the man was who called here? I'm wondering if it was the same one who saw my pa. Was he a local man, and was he buying up spreads for himself or someone else?'

'I can't answer those questions, but Pa might be able to. Will you stay and eat with us?'

'I don't know. I picked up a man who was trailing me here. He busted out of prison with Jack Tate.'

'If anyone knows what's going on around here it will be Tate,' Jane affirmed. 'Have you talked to him yet?'

'I'll get round to him shortly.' Lew moved to a window and looked out at the yard. He saw Tulse standing by the corral with Joe Wishart and the two cowboys, and judging by their attitudes it looked as if Tulse was having a hard time. 'I want to hear what Tulse is saying,' he mused. 'Where's Wayne?'

'He's here in the house. I wouldn't want any of the locals to find out he's up and about again. As far as most folk know, Wayne is still being treated back East.'

Lew left the house and crossed to the corral. One of the cowboys was covering Tulse with a pistol while Wishart asked questions. Tulse was shaking his head emphatically and denying any knowledge of local trouble. The questioning stopped when Lew reached them, and Wishart shook his head.

'We're wasting our time with him, Lew,' he said. 'He's a hardcase and will keep his lip buttoned till hell freezes over. He must know something of what's going on.'

'We should bury him up to his neck and leave him for the sun to bake.' Appleton, a big fleshy man in his forties, had hard blue eyes, and spoke from the right side of his mouth because of a livid scar which ran from the right corner of his mouth to the lobe of his right ear. 'And I'd sure like to dig the hole to put him in. Elrington was worth ten of him, and I ain't keen on this feller being handed to the local law.'

'I could spill some of the things Jack Tate told me in prison,' Tulse said desperately. 'He sure played up hell around here before they put him behind bars.'

'What sort of things?' Lew demanded.

'I'll do a deal with you. Turn me loose afterwards and I'll give you the whole works.'

'You've got yourself a deal,' Lew spoke without hesitation, 'but it better be the real McCoy.'

'Tate killed a man named Harper.' Tulse looked warily at Lew. 'I guess it must have been your father.'

Lew felt an icy pang stab through his chest, and clenched his hands convulsively.

'Tell me more,' he said, 'and give it to me straight.'

'The man was Frank Harper. He owned the Circle H spread.'

'You're talking about my father,' Lew grated. 'What happened?'

'They cheated him out of his ranch, and when he left with the money from the sale they sent Jack Tate after him to get the dough back and kill him so he couldn't cause trouble.'

'When was this?' Wishart demanded.

'It was while Tate was in the jail in Bostock for shooting your brother, but they let him out one night to do the job, and he went back to jail afterwards.'

'Who was the sheriff in town at that time?' Lew asked Wishart.

'You might well ask.' Wishart spoke through his teeth. 'It was Buck Shenton.' He spat in disgust. 'Now we're getting to know what we're up against.'

'The deal was that Tate would go to prison and get busted out later,' Tulse said eagerly, 'to come out to a pile of dough for his time and trouble.'

'Did Tate say where he buried my father?' Lew demanded.

'No, he never said.' Tulse shook his head.

'What did he have to say about shooting my brother Wayne?'

'He shot your brother for the same reason he killed your father. He was always bragging about what he'd done. He wanted everyone to think he was a real tough cuss.'

'So what did he say about Wayne?'

'He had to kill him to clear the way for getting at your father. They didn't want any loose ends after they got the old man.'

'Who are they – the men you're talking about?' Lew demanded. 'Who's buying up the ranches, and why?'

'That I can't say. But I've given you enough to go on. Tate was working for Casey Mitchell before he went into jail, and Shenton let him out for the night when your father was killed. You should be able to learn more from either of them. Now how about turning me loose? I'll head out of the county and never come back.'

'Can you hold him here on the ranch while I look into what he's said?' Lew asked Wishart.

'Yeah, just for a few days. We'll take care of him. But

how are you gonna get the truth from Tate or Shenton or Mitchell? You said Tate is back in jail with a bullet hole in him, and what can you do against a county sheriff? It's obvious now that you'll need proof of his wrongdoing, and I reckon he's covered his tracks pretty well. As for Mitchell, he runs a tough outfit there in town. I don't think you'd get him to talk, not in a hundred years.'

'I'll work something out,' Lew said. 'I'll head back to town and nose around. I've got one or two ideas, and there are a couple of pointers I want to check out. What I'd really like to know about is why ranches are being bought up. You said it started with Herb Bean and Bert Sadler selling out and leaving. Then it was our place, and now someone's making a move on you, Joe. Jane told me about the man who showed up last week wanting you to sell out to him.'

'That sidewinder!' Wishart cursed. 'I don't know who he was. As soon as I heard his offer I ran him out of the yard. He wasn't local; I don't know where he came from.'

'It's a pity you didn't find out,' Lew said. 'I need all the information I can get.'

'He might show up again,' Wishart said hopefully, 'and if he does I'll work on him. Boys, put Tulse in the store-room and lock the door. That'll hold him. You'll behave yourself, Tulse, if you wanta get out of here alive.'

'Anything you say,' Tulse said eagerly.

'There's one more thing,' Lew said, and Tulse caught his breath. 'Who was at the Circle H when Nolan sent you and Tate out for Elrington and me in that copse?'

'I don't know their names, but there were two men with Nolan when we rode in. One of them was nursing a bullet wound. They talked about a gun trap they set in town the day before that failed.'

'Are you sure there were no more than three in there?' Lew persisted.

'I didn't see anyone else.' Tulse shook his head emphatically.

'I'll come back for you if I find you've been lying to me, and you'll never leave here,' Lew told him, and with that, went back into the house.

'Will you stay and eat with us?' Jane offered.

Lew shook his head. 'Thanks, but no thanks. I need to get back to town to talk to Jack Tate. I just learned that he killed my father three years ago.'

Jane's face froze into a mask of shock and she caught her breath.

'Are you sure Tate did that?' she demanded.

'I'll make sure before I kill him,' Lew replied savagely, and went out to his horse. He rode off without looking back, an intolerable weight of grief and guilt occupying his mind.

# SEVEN

Buck Shenton sneaked into the livery barn and stood just inside the back door to check the interior. Satisfied that he was alone, he eased towards the stable office and peered in at the door. Ed Faylen was seated behind his desk; the contents of the whiskey bottle in front of him had diminished considerably since Hanks had been taken away to jail. Faylen was badly shaken by the shooting of Pete Elrington and his nerves were in revolt. When he saw Shenton peering in at the office doorway he almost jumped out of his skin, and started up from the desk.

'What do you want now, Sheriff?' he demanded. 'There's nothing more I can tell you.'

'I know enough already.' Shenton grinned. He cast a glance over his shoulder to the open front doorway, which was deserted. It was a quiet time of the day. 'I've got something to show you, Ed,' he added disarmingly. 'Come and take a look.'

Frowning, Faylen followed Shenton out of the office. The sheriff walked towards the rear door, and Faylen caught up with him as Shenton turned to look around once more. The livery barn was otherwise deserted.

'What's going on?' Faylen demanded.

'You've been stepping out of line.' Shenton pushed Faylen roughly and the liveryman staggered backwards into an empty stall. His heels caught on an obstruction; he lost his balance and fell on a pile of straw. He looked up at Shenton, who had drawn his pistol and was lunging at him, face twisted into a mask of violence. Faylen opened his mouth to cry out but the sheriff's pistol swung viciously in a small arc and the barrel slammed against the side of Faylen's head. Blackness denser than the darkest night slipped in front of Faylen's eyes and he gasped and lost consciousness. Shenton struck again for good measure before checking the liveryman, and he grinned when he found Faylen was dead, his skull broken.

Shenton went out the back door and passed the corral to look into a smaller barn. His eyes glinted when he saw the half-wild black stallion that Faylen kept separate from his other stock. The black had a reputation of being a killer, which was the attraction at the weekends when cowboys from outlying ranches congregated around the corral to try their skill and strength against the stallion. No one had ever succeeded in riding the horse, but that fact only increased their determination to try, and Faylen made a lot of money laying odds against the punchers gaining mastery over the beast. Doc Allen was kept busy most weekends, setting broken arms or legs and doctoring bruises and sprains.

Shenton took a hackamore from a post and put in on the stallion before opening the stall. The horse was like a docile mare, until someone tried to get astride its back.

Shenton led it into the barn and turned it into the stall where Faylen was lying. He closed the gate and slipped the hackamore off the animal's head, and then whipped it with the rope. The stallion objected to the rough treatment and tried to bite Shenton, who backed off. Shenton struck the animal again and it backed away until it touched Faylen with its rear feet. The horse lashed out with both steel-shod hoofs, and then whirled, snorting and trumpeting, to stomp the lifeless body under its feet.

The sheriff turned away, highly satisfied, and went out to the corral. He mounted his horse and rode out for the Box W. He needed now to kill Lew Harper. . . .

Lew rode from Box W in a cold sweat. He wanted to get to grips with the bunch causing all the local trouble, and in particular he wanted to see Jack Tate and Buck Shenton through gunsmoke. But as he rode towards town his emotions settled and he began to consider his options. He could not afford to go up against Shenton while the man held the office of sheriff, and he could not get at Tate unless he went through Shenton. He considered the rest of what he had learned and came to the conclusion that his best bet would be to revisit Circle H and grab the two men who had set the gun trap in town.

He topped a rise, saw a rider approaching, and slipped back over the crest. He rode to his right, dismounted and trailed his reins. He watched Buck Shenton pass by, apparently heading for Box W, and wondered what the crooked sheriff was up to. He struggled against the impulse to attack Shenton, and watched him disappear over a ridge. He guessed Joe Wishart could handle anything that Shenton might try, and rode on to Circle H.

The sun was low in the western sky by the time Lew reined in and looked down on his former home. He saw Nolan and another man out by the corral, tending horses. He recalled the faces of the two men he had seen sitting outside the saloon when he had ridden into town and knew the second man was one of those who had set the gun trap. He remained in cover until the pair returned to the house. Smoke was coming from a stovepipe, and Lew guessed that the third man, who had been wounded in the gun trap, was probably lying up in the house.

Lew left his horse in cover and entered the ranch by way of the barn. He moved warily, his senses fully alert, his right hand close to the butt of his gun. His mind was filled with a discordant clamour as he tried to come to terms with the grim news of his father's death. Anger flooded him in waves, and he sweated at the thought of the crookedness flourishing on his home range. But he consoled himself with the certain knowledge that his time would come, and then the badmen would pay for their crimes with their lives.

He entered the barn by the back door and looked around intently. Nothing seemed to have changed during his absence, and he could almost believe that all he had to do was walk into the ranch house to find his father alive and well. He paused by a post just inside the big front door and saw his initials in the soft wood where he had carved them in happier times. He clenched his hands and fought the grief-laden rage that swept through him until it faded and he could breathe easily.

There was an open space between the barn and the back of the house. Lew drew his pistol and checked its load. Eagerness began flaring through his breast like yeast rising in a baking loaf. He set out across the back yard, his face pulled into a grimace of determination. This was where he started paying debts for his father.

The back door to the house was locked. Lew peered into the kitchen through a small window beside the door. The kitchen was empty, although a large pot was steaming on the stove.

Lew thought for a moment. Three-to-one were long odds in a stand-up fight, so he would have to sneak in and get the drop on these men. He moved around to the left side of the house and came to the window of the room his father had used as an office. Knowing the house intimately, he was aware that the catch on the office window had always been faulty. He tried it and discovered that it had not been repaired during his absence. He slid the window open and climbed into the house.

Voices were talking somewhere in the front part of the house, and someone laughed raucously. Lew palmed his gun and cocked it. He went forward to the door that gave access to the large front living room; the voices came plainly through the closed door. He opened the door silently and stepped quickly into the room. Nolan was standing in front of the big fireplace, a second man was seated in his father's favourite leather armchair, and a third man, his chest heavily bandaged, was lying on a couch under one of the porch windows.

Lew coughed to attract attention and startled eyes swung to gaze at him.

'Just stand still and don't do anything with your hands,' Lew rapped.

Nolan instinctively dropped his hand to his holstered gun, but stopped the movement instantly. He raised his hands, his bruised face pulling into a silent snarl as he recognized Lew. The wounded man lifted his hands into the air without being told, and remained motionless. The third man spread his hands and held them away from his pistol.

'Very sensible,' Lew remarked. 'Nobody moves unless I say so. Nolan, draw your pistol with just your forefinger and thumb. Throw it into the far corner. We've got some unfinished business to settle, and I'll get around to you shortly.' He paused while Nolan got rid of his weapon, and then looked at the second man. 'What's your name?' He waggled his gun menacingly. 'You tried to kill me yesterday in a gun trap at the stable in town.'

'I'm Miller,' the man growled 'and I didn't try to kill anyone. I wasn't even in town yesterday.'

'Stand up and dump your gun. Keep your trap shut unless I ask you questions.'

Miller drew his gun and tossed it into the far corner. He remained standing, his hands clear of his body, but there was a wolfish expression on his face that spoke of desperation, and Lew recognized it for what it was. Lew turned his attention to the wounded man on the couch, recalling the fleshy face from the picture that was etched in his mind of two men sitting on seats outside the saloon in town. He readily recognized both men, and sight of a Stetson lying on the floor beside the couch with the hat brim pinned up at the front by a thorn thrust through it confirmed his suspicion that these were the two men he had seen.

'I wasn't in town either,' the wounded man said in a

throaty voice before Lew could accuse him.

'What's your name?' Lew demanded.

'I'm Buster Nelson.'

'How'd you get shot?'

'It was an accident. Miller was cleaning his gun yesterday and it went off.'

'So neither of you was in town yesterday, huh?' Lew asked.

Both men agreed hurriedly.

'Then how come I saw both of you sitting outside the saloon in town when I rode in?' Lew shook his head. 'Don't bother denying it. I spoke to a witness in the saloon and he described both of you. So why are you lying?' He grimaced, and answered the question himself. 'To cover up the truth, that's why. But your lies won't wash. I know a lot about what's going on around here. Nolan, I've come back to ask you some more questions, and remember what happened when you didn't want to talk yesterday – there's plenty more of that to come.'

'You'll be wasting your time,' Nolan growled. 'I don't know anything.'

Lew walked over to Nolan and paused just out of arm's reach. 'Turn around,' he ordered.

Nolan hesitated as if he knew what was coming. He shook his head. 'I ain't gonna turn my back on you,' he snarled.

Lew slid his left foot forward a half pace and his left fist shot out in a powerful arc. His knuckles cracked against Nolan's jaw and the big man went down heavily, striking his head on the fireplace before dropping to the floor. Lew eased the hammer of his gun forward and bent to slam the barrel against Nolan's right temple. He straightened quickly as he caught a movement from Miller, and saw the man lunging to tackle him. He cocked his gun again.

'Are you tired of living?' Lew demanded. Miller froze. 'Let me tell you that I know my father was murdered by the men you three are working for, and I plan to collect from all of them. So now you know you're right up against it. I'm gonna ask questions, and I want the right answers, or else. Do you understand what I'm saying?'

'I ain't killed anyone,' Nelson said. 'You wouldn't shoot an innocent man.'

'My father was innocent, but Jack Tate killed him,' Lew replied relentlessly.

'Shenton took Tate to town and jailed him,' Miller cut in. 'If you want him all you've got to do is go in there and take him.'

'I'll get to both of them later. Miller, get that lariat off the wall over there and tie Nolan. Do a good job because I'll check your knots. Then you can tie Nelson.'

Miller obeyed without question, working feverishly while throwing an occasional troubled glance at Lew, who checked Nolan and Nelson when Miller had finished.

Lew turned his attention to Miller, who was looking uneasy.

'So who told you and Nelson to come into town yesterday and lay for me?' he asked.

Miller shrugged, and a dogged expression came into his dark eyes as he shook his head. 'No one told us anything,' he replied.

'There was only Nolan here,' Lew observed. 'So he gave

the order, huh?'

'If you know that then why ask me?' Miller countered.

'I want to trace that order back to its source.' Lew went to where Miller was standing. Miller frowned and stepped back a pace, half lifting his hands as if preparing to defend himself despite Lew's levelled gun.

'It was Nolan told us,' Nelson said, and Lew transferred his attention to the wounded man.

'Nelson, you better button your lip,' Miller rasped.

'It's all right for you,' Nelson protested. 'You ain't got a bullet hole in your chest and you ain't hogtied. Me, I want out of this. I've had enough.'

'So tell me what's going on around here,' Lew said sharply. 'Give me some answers and I'll take you into Bostock so the doc can look you over. I might even turn you loose if I'm happy with your answers.'

'Nolan said to ride into town yesterday when you left, and lay for you.' Nelson was sweating, and his lips quivered. 'He runs things around here, and Hanks is often out this way with new orders.'

'So what orders did Hanks bring here yesterday, and who were they from?'

'Nelson, keep your mouth shut,' Miller warned again.

'You open your mouth again, and you'll chew on my gun barrel,' Lew told Miller. 'It'll be your turn to talk shortly.'

'Hanks works at the bank in town.' Nelson stifled a groan as he tried to change his position on the couch. 'I guess he takes his orders from the banker. I wouldn't know what happens away from this place. I guess you'll have to ask Shenton or Mitchell.'

'Two ranches were bought out before my father was killed and this spread got taken over,' Lew mused. 'Now the same process is starting against Box W. What's behind the take-overs?'

'We only take orders,' Miller said. 'It's no use asking us questions like that. What the hell do we know? Pick on Mitchell or Shenton. They live in a bigger pool than us. We're small fry compared to them.'

Lew turned quickly and struck Miller a blow with his gun. Miller groaned and fell on his face. Lew tied him hand and foot with the rest of the lariat and then turned his attention to Nolan, who had recovered his senses and was watching him from his position in front of the fire-place.

'So I come back to you, Nolan,' Lew said. 'Who do you get your orders from?'

'Go to hell,' Nolan rasped. 'I ain't talking about nothing.'

'You're standing right on the brink,' Lew said, waggling his pistol with the muzzle under Nolan's nose. 'My father has been murdered, and I'm not gonna pussyfoot around. I want the men responsible. I know Jack Tate shot my father, but I want the men who gave him his orders. I don't care who I get the information from, but anyone who won't give me answers when I ask questions is asking to be pushed over the edge.'

'You don't scare me,' Nolan snarled. 'Kill me, and you won't get any answers at all.'

Lew realized that he was not going to make any progress with these men. They did not know enough about the situation to be able to give him the background to the trouble. He would have to do as Nolan suggested and go for the men higher up in the organization. But what was he to do with his prisoners in the meantime? If he turned them loose they would either pull out while the going was good or run to their immediate boss and report the development, which would probably cause a full-scale hunt to be made for him, which would end only with his death.

At that moment Lew heard the sound of hoofs out in the yard, and ran to a porch window to see who was arriving. . . .

Buck Shenton was thoughtful as he rode to Box W. He was satisfied with the way he had killed the liveryman, Faylen, but there was a niggling doubt in the back of his mind that had begun to make its presence felt when Lew Harper had ridden into Bostock the day before. He could not put his finger on the reason for it, but felt ill at ease, as if something important had been overlooked in the planning of the takeover of the ranches that could ultimately bring about the downfall of the whole scheme. It had to do with Lew Harper, but the exact nature of the premonition did not readily reveal itself to his agile mind, and he tried, without success, to puzzle out the reason by a process of elimination and conjecture. When he was unable to pinpoint the problem his indecision made him irritable.

When he came in sight of Box W he reined in and studied the ranch for some minutes, wondering how far he should go in trying to get Joe Wishart to change his mind about not selling the ranch. It was not good policy to have too many dead people on the range. He had not been around when the Harper ranch had been taken over, but the fact that loose ends had been left, to the detriment of the general scheme, was borne out by the unexpected return of Lew Harper, who would have to be killed as soon as possible. But Harper was turning out to be a man who would not easily be put down.

He saw Joe Wishart emerge from the house and pause on the porch to look around. He wondered why Harper had ridden out here, although it was obvious that he was trying to unearth details of what had happened during his absence from the range. He realized that it all came down to Harper. There was no knowing what other loose ends had been left around, and Harper seemed to be a man who would stop at nothing to get what he wanted. The missing Frank Harper was a goad to his son, and Shenton knew that nothing short of a fatal bullet would end Lew Harper's search for him.

Shenton touched spurs to his horse and rode into the ranch yard. Wishart straightened and gazed at him as he reined in. Shenton studied Wishart's face and manner, looking for pointers to his attitude. Wishart had been visited twice and sounded out about selling the ranch, and there was a set to his pugnacious jaw, which pointed to his determination not to be bullied or manipulated in any way. But that was to be expected in a man who had no plans to sell his livelihood. So he would have to be scared into accepting a different point of view.

'What do you want, Sheriff?' Wishart demanded.

'I was out this way so I thought I'd drop by and check that everything is OK. I'm looking for Lew Harper, and I figured he might be here.'

'He was here earlier, but rode out again. Why do you want him?'

'I need to talk to him, that's all. You sound as if you expect me to arrest him on sight.' Shenton smiled briefly. 'Did he tell you that Jack Tate broke out of prison and showed up at the Circle H?' Shenton continued. 'Harper rode out to the home ranch, where Tate attacked him and was shot. Harper brought Tate to town to the doctor; I've got Tate in jail now. You've heard, no doubt, that there was some trouble at the livery barn, and Hanks, the bank guard, shot Pete Elrington. I've got Hanks behind bars too.'

'I heard all about it. Lew should have killed those rattlers stone dead. Tate has been nothing but trouble all his life. As for Hanks – why did he kill Pete?'

'I don't know that yet.' Shenton shook his head.

'I was gonna come into town and talk to you about some trouble I've been getting.' Wishart grimaced. 'There's been a man out here to see me a couple of times about selling the spread. I ran him off the place the last time he showed up. What he was offering for the ranch was a steal, and since he's been around I've been getting trouble. Nothing much to shake a stick at, but a few head of cattle have disappeared, and someone burned down my shack on the west line.'

'Have you seen anyone prowling around?' Shenton asked. 'And who was the man who offered to buy you out? Did he come from around here or was he a stranger?'

'He was a stranger to me. I'd never set eyes on him before. But I'll sure know him again.'

'I'll have to get a deputy.' Shenton shrugged. 'If there's

trouble coming then I'll need some help.'

'Trouble coming? Hell, there's been trouble around here for years and nothing has been done about it. Frank Harper disappeared, and no one found out why. His son Wayne was shot and nearly killed, and no one has discovered why Jack Tate did it. Lew Harper came back home and has been shot a couple of times. So what is going on around here? Either you ain't doing your job properly, Sheriff, or there's more to this trouble than we know about.'

'What do you mean?' Shenton demanded. 'Are you saying you think I know what's going on and not doing anything about it?'

'So you do know something's going on,' Wishart rasped.

'I didn't say that!' Shenton countered.

Wishart thought of the information that Tulse had given Lew only that morning about Tate's bragging in prison, and he believed it to be true, which pointed to the fact that Shenton had let Tate out of jail to shoot Frank Harper. Wishart fought an impulse to blurt out the truth and get Shenton's reaction, but he was aware that such a confrontation could end in shooting, with him on the receiving end. He shook his head and held his tongue, wanting to do something but fearful of the consequences.

But Shenton was not satisfied. 'I don't like the way you're talking,' he said.

'It's obvious there's a land-grab going on.' Wishart began to get hot under the collar. The death of Pete Elrington was rankling in his mind. He had seen three ranches change hands in the last three years, and sensed that he was next on the list, unless he made a stand. 'What do you know about the men handling the deal? And have you taken steps to find Frank Harper?'

'You're talking through the back of your neck. You don't have any idea how I've tried to get to the bottom of what's been happening.' Shenton dropped his hand to the butt of his gun but did not draw the weapon. He saw Wishart step back a pace, and the rancher's face changed expression, as if he feared getting shot. The impulse to draw and fire at Wishart flared through Shenton's mind and he had to struggle to stay his hand, although his desire shone balefully in his eyes.

'Am I to be shot too?' Wishart demanded. He was unarmed, and wished he had buckled on his gun-belt before emerging from the house.

'Are you hinting that I've shot someone?' Shenton palmed his gun with a fluid movement, levelled it at the rancher, and then stuck the muzzle against Wishart's chest. Wishart backed against the wall of the house and Shenton closed with him. Wishart reached up with both hands and grasped Shenton's gun barrel. Shenton gritted his teeth and tried to jerk the weapon away from the rancher, but Wishart hung on, trying to twist the weapon out of Shenton's hand. The gun was hair-triggered, and the twisting motion applied by Wishart caused Shenton's finger to put pressure on the trigger. The gun blasted instantly, and a slug hammered into Wishart's chest.

Wishart yelled and fell to the porch. Shenton gazed down at him and saw blood pulsing out of the wound. He lowered his muzzle and fired again, aiming at Wishart's head. The bullet struck the rancher between the eyes and blew off the back of his skull. Blood sprayed over the porch. Shenton looked around. He saw a cowpuncher over by the corral, watched the man's head jerk around at the sound of the shot and glance towards the house. He stopped what he was doing and came running across the yard to the porch, drawing a pistol as he did so.

Shenton bared his teeth in a mirthless grin, threw down on the puncher, and squeezed the trigger twice. The cowboy stopped as if he had run into the side of a barn and dropped in his tracks. A bullet smacked into a porch post beside Shenton's head and he looked around to see a second cowboy standing in front of the bunkhouse door.

Shenton tried a long shot. His slug struck woodwork close to the cowboy. The man retreated into the bunkhouse and Shenton ran into the house. He recalled Fenner's words that Joe Wishart should be killed and his daughter Jane left to handle the ranch. He looked in the big kitchen, which was deserted, and as he turned to search the rest of the house he heard someone kicking at the inside of the storeroom door off the rear of the kitchen. Gun in hand, he went to investigate, and pushed the door open to find Tulse inside.

'Who are you and what the hell are you doing locked in here?' Shenton demanded.

Tulse saw Shenton's badge, looked at the levelled gun, and hurried to explain.

'I'm one of the men who escaped from prison with Jack Tate,' he said. 'Tate told me you were on our side. I got picked up by Lew Harper and brought here. Wishart was holding me until Harper comes back. I think Harper's on his way to Circle H.'

'The hell you say.' Shenton paused and listened intently but there were no sounds in the big house, and he guessed that Jane Wishart was hiding under the bed, or something. But he had no business with her at the moment. 'Come on, Tulse. We'd better get after Harper and stop his hunting around.'

They went out to the porch. Shenton stepped up into his saddle.

'I need a horse,' Tulse said, and ducked when a bullet smacked into the wall beside him. 'Who is that over there?

'Get a gun out of the house and cover me from here,' Shenton said. 'I'll ride around to the back of the bunkhouse and nail that other puncher.'

He set off as Tulse ran into the house, circled the barn, and approached the bunkhouse from the rear. Appleton was inside, covering the ranch house from the front window. Shenton dismounted and trailed his reins. He moved silently along the side of the bunkhouse to the front left corner and eased along the front wall towards a glassless window. He could see the barrel of a Winchester protruding from the aperture, and, when he was close enough, reached out and grasped it with his left hand. He jerked the long gun from Appleton's hands, thrust the muzzle of his Colt through the window, and blasted two shots into the cowpuncher's chest.

Tulse came running across the yard and entered the corral to saddle up his horse. Shenton climbed back into his saddle and spurred the horse. Tulse joined him and they galloped across the yard towards the gate. As they passed the house a gun fired at them. Shenton glanced around, saw Jane Wishart's pale face peering through a window, and heard the crash of another shot as the girl cut loose at them. He turned away, urging his horse on to greater effort, and headed fast for Circle H, aware that it was high time he got rid of Lew Harper. . . .

# EIGHT

Lew looked out the front window of the Circle H ranch house and saw two riders approaching. He recognized Shenton immediately, and frowned because he was not yet ready to confront the crooked sheriff. When he recognized Tulse as the second rider his heart lurched, and he was filled with disbelief; Tulse was supposed to be locked in Wishart's storeroom at the Box W. He moved back from the window, his mind turning over the possibilities, and then headed for the kitchen door. He could not afford a confrontation with Shenton because the lawman had the full weight of the law behind him. He ran from the house, dashed to the barn, and passed through it to get to his horse at the rear. As he rode away he heard a shot, but reached an adjacent rise without incident. He dismounted in cover and settled down to watch the ranch.

Silence enveloped Lew and nothing moved around the ranch. He sweated under the strong sun, lying unmoving in lush grass, his eyes shaded from the glare by the wide brim of his Stetson. But while he was motionless, his thoughts whirling with conjecture, a number of questions filled his mind. How had Tulse managed to escape from Box W? And what was he doing in the company of the crooked sheriff? Lew recalled seeing Shenton riding towards the Wishart ranch after he had left it, and now his thoughts took on a darker shade as he tried to imagine what had occurred there when the sheriff had arrived.

Movement in the back yard of the ranch attracted his gaze and he grimaced when Nolan and Miller ran from the kitchen door of the house to the corral and began saddling their horses. Moments later, Shenton and Tulse rode into view from the front of the house and made for the corral. As soon as Nolan and Miller were ready to travel, the four men checked for tracks, and then began to trail towards the spot where Lew was waiting and watching.

Lew got up and went back to his horse. He mounted and set out fast, wanting to avoid a fight with Shenton. He had somehow to discredit the crooked sheriff before attempting to put him down. When he broke cover he was spotted immediately, and shots were fired at him, although he was well out of range. He glanced back and saw the four riders spurring their horses towards him, and knew that he was in for a long, hard run. He spurred his horse for greater speed, aware that Shenton needed to shut his mouth before he could tell anyone what he had learned.

The horse Lew had bought from Faylen soon proved to be short on stamina. After three miles at a gallop the animal began to labour, and its breath whistled and wheezed in its throat. Lew looked over his shoulder, saw that Shenton and Nolan were gaining on him while Miller and Tulse were having trouble keeping up. He realized that he had to hole up somewhere and fight them off. He knew this range like the back of his hand, and tried to think of a place where he might have a good chance of chasing them away, but he had second thoughts as he considered that Shenton could easily fake a crime against him and kill him legally for resisting arrest.

He turned instinctively in the direction of Box W – the only place in the county where he could expect to get some help. Joe Wishart would be having trouble now, and they could support each other. When shooting started again, and he heard bullets thudding into the ground about him, he looked back and saw that Shenton and Nolan had closed on him considerably and were endeavouring to get his range. He tried to coax more speed out of his flagging horse but the animal had given its best and could not maintain its already failing progress. Lew expected it to drop in its tracks at any moment.

Lew breasted a rise and reined in to dismount as soon as he was in cover. He dragged his Winchester from the saddle-boot and levered a cartridge into the breech as he dropped to the ground and crawled back up to the crest. Shenton and Nolan were spurring their mounts, almost shoulder to shoulder in their eagerness to make a quick kill. Lew lifted the rifle to his shoulder and glanced through the back sight. His foresight settled on Nolan and he fired. He saw Nolan slide sideways out of his saddle, hit the ground hard, and then bounce a couple of times before slumping into an inert heap.

Shenton hauled on his reins and dived out of his saddle before Lew could draw a bead on him. The crooked sheriff vanished into low ground, but did not open fire at

Lew's position. Lew eased back a fraction and waited for a sight of Shenton, but the sheriff was too cunning to expose himself. Gun echoes drifted away across the range. Nolan did not move, and Lew wondered if he had killed the man. Minutes later, while still watching for signs of Shenton, he saw Miller and Tulse coming up, and decided it was time to get moving again. He waited until Tulse was in range and fired at him. Tulse vacated his saddle and rolled into cover. Lew grinned tightly, aware that he was the master of this situation; he had the high ground and they were off their horses.

He watched as Miller rode back out of range. There was still no sign of Shenton. Lew shook his head and slid back off the crest. He ran to his horse, vaulted into the saddle, thrust his rifle into its boot and then rode on, heading for Box W.

Buck Shenton stayed down in the depression and listened to the fading echoes of the shooting. He had respect for Lew's abilities, and was aware that he had to concentrate on killing Lew before thinking of anything else. Minutes passed in absolute silence, and he began to think that Lew had pulled out, but did not stick up his head to check his hunch. It was not until Miller rode up without drawing fire from the ridge that Shenton got to his feet and looked around. Tulse was out of his saddle and bending over the inert Nolan. A moment later, Nolan sat up.

'So what do we do now, Sheriff?' Miller demanded.

'We keep right on after Harper, what else? He's got to be killed. He's beginning to put two and two together, and if he passes on what he's learning then we'll all be for the high jump. Fetch my horse, Miller, and let's get moving.'

Miller brought Shenton's horse to him and the sheriff climbed into his saddle. He rode back to where Nolan was standing shakily and looked down at the big man.

'Are you OK?' he demanded.

'Gimme a minute and I will be,' Nolan replied. 'Are we going after Harper?'

'What else? We have to put him down.'

'That's your job, or Jack Tate's,' said Miller, coming up.

'Yeah, I forgot.' Shenton grinned crookedly. 'You only shoot men in the back or from cover and you can't even do that properly. But Harper is proving hard to kill. I reckon it ain't a one-man job, so I need some help on this one. We're gonna ride him down and finish him before he blows the whistle on us. Come on, let's get moving. He's getting away while we're wagging our chins.'

They spread out and advanced up the ridge. When they reached the crest they saw Lew in the distance, riding steadily towards Box W.

'He bought that old hay burner from Faylen,' Shenton mused, 'and it looks like it's on its last legs. Come on, let's go nail him. I need to get back to town and make a report on what's been happening. In fact, on second thoughts, I reckon you three can go for Harper while I head back to Bostock. And don't any of you give up. Keep on until you kill Harper. Have you got that?'

'How about if he gets to Box W before we catch up with him?' Nolan demanded. 'We could be in a lot of trouble if we ride in there.'

'You won't be,' Shenton reassured him. 'I took care of Wishart and his men before I came on here, so get to it

118

and do a good job. Come on back to town when Harper is dead.'

They rode out at a fast pace and Shenton sat his horse to watch them, hoping the three of them could handle Harper. He waited until they disappeared from sight and then rode back towards Circle H, heading for town. He was bypassing the ranch when a thought struck him and he entered the yard to dismount in front of the porch. Buster Nelson called out when Shenton opened the front door, and he peered into the big room to see Nelson sitting up on the couch with a pistol in his hand.

'Oh, it's you!' Nelson lowered his gun. 'I thought Harper had come back. That guy sure is hell on wheels! Where are the others? Has Harper killed them?'

'Harper will be dead before sundown,' Shenton said. 'He's running for the Box W, but the boys will get him. I thought you were cashing in your chips, Buster.' Shenton walked to Nelson's side and reached down to take the gun from Nelson's hand. 'You look healthy enough to me, which is a pity. I've got to rig a murder to pin on Harper in case the boys don't get him; you're elected as his victim.'

'What the hell!' Nelson's expression changed as he caught Shenton's meaning. 'Say, you ain't thinking of bumping me off, are you?' he demanded.

'Say your prayers, Buster.' Shenton stepped back a couple of paces and levelled the gun.

Nelson held up a hand as if trying to ward off a bullet.

'So long, sucker.' Shenton squeezed the trigger, and the .45 bullet smacked into the centre of Nelson's chest, the impact throwing him across the couch. The crash of the

119

shot reverberated in the room. Shenton remained motionless until the echoes faded, then tossed the gun down
beside Nelson's body and departed. He climbed into his
saddle and set out for town.

Before he had covered another mile, Lew knew that his
mount would not make the trip to Box W at anything
faster than a canter. He glanced back over his shoulder,
saw three riders following him, and realized they were
getting closer by the minute. He noted that Shenton was
not in sight, and wondered if the sheriff was circling him
to get ahead. The thought pushed him into action and he
looked around for an ambush spot. He left the trail and
headed for high ground. Shooting started up behind him
and the sound of closely passing slugs made him set his
spurs into the flanks of his struggling horse.

He had almost reached the crest of a ridge when his
horse faltered and pulled up. Lew dismounted quickly and
took his Winchester from the saddle-boot. He ran up the
slope to gain the crest as his pursuers redoubled their
efforts to shoot him, and when he finally threw himself
down in cover his wounded leg and shoulder were throbbing with pain.

Miller, Nolan and Tulse rode into cover at the bottom
of the slope. Tulse started shooting at the crest with his
rifle. Nolan set off to the right, intending to outflank the
ridge, and he motioned to Miller to accompany him. Lew
watched them disappearing into cover to his left and
guessed their intention. He watched Tulse, saw the man
appear and fire a shot, then duck down, and he timed the
interval between Tulse's up and down movements. He was
ready when Tulse appeared again, and fired before Tulse

could take aim. Tulse had not bothered to change his position, but Lew was centred on him, and fired the instant he saw Tulse's head showing.

Tulse never knew what hit him. He saw Lew's head and shoulders above the crest and made a minor adjustment to his aim, but at that moment Lew's bullet hit him between the eyes. He felt no pain as blackness enveloped him, and his lifeless body sprawled backwards. Lew moved instantly, drew back off the ridge, and got to his feet. He looked in the direction Nolan and Miller had gone, saw no sign of them, and started down the slope to where the trio had left their horses. He needed another mount, and if he could collect the three horses at the bottom of the slope he would leave Nolan and Miller afoot.

Nolan paused when he heard no further shots, and looked questioningly at Miller.

'Do you think Tulse has pulled out?' he demanded.

'More likely got himself killed.' Miller grimaced. 'We'd better get back there and check.'

They retraced their steps, and were in time to see Lew disappearing into the depression at the bottom of the slope where they had left their horses. Nolan cursed and started running towards the spot. Miller halted and lifted his rifle to cover the place where he expected Lew to show. A moment later three horses appeared. Lew was riding one of the mounts and leading the other two. Miller opened fire. His first shot hit one of the lead horses and it went down with threshing hoofs, dragging its reins from Lew's hand. Lew hunched over in the saddle of Nolan's horse to minimize his target area. The bay was a powerful animal, and lengthened its stride as Lew raked it with his spurs.

Nolan halted and stood cursing as Lew vanished into the distance. He looked at Lew's horse, standing forlornly on the slope, and scowled as Miller approached him.

'You'll have to ride that crowbait back to the ranch and pick up a couple of fresh mounts for us,' he said heavily. 'I'll wait here until you get back.'

Miller shook his head wordlessly and went to fetch Lew's horse. The animal could barely canter when he mounted it, and he used his spurs without success.

Lew had ridden east of the trail to Box W in an attempt to throw off pursuit, and now adjusted his direction, but when he was out of sight of Nolan and Miller he turned the horse and rode along his back trail until he could observe the two men. He saw Miller riding in the direction of Circle W and waited until he was out of sight. Nolan sat down on a knoll. Lew rode towards him, drawing his pistol and keeping Nolan covered as he approached.

Nolan did not hear the bay's hoofs in the lush grass until Lew was almost upon him. He sprang up and swung around when he heard an unnatural sound, but by then he was at a disadvantage. Lew was only a dozen yards away, with a levelled gun steady in his right hand and an expression on his face which boded ill for Nolan.

Cleaver Nolan reached for his holstered Colt in a fast movement. The weapon was almost clear of leather when he realized he had no chance of beating Lew so he stopped his draw and let go of the gun. The weapon fell to the ground. Lew reined in and stepped down from the saddle, keeping Nolan covered.

'Step away from that gun,' Lew commanded. He moved forward as Nolan obeyed. 'I guess you've come to the end of your trail, mister,' he continued. 'You've been trying to kill me so it's time I put you out of your misery. If I let you go you'll only come after me again, and I don't need you under my feet.'

'Hold your fire,' Nolan rasped. 'Don't do anything right now. I'll make a deal with you. Stick me in the town jail afterwards if you like, but don't shoot.'

'Do I look like something that crawled out from under a rock?' Lew demanded. 'You'd like to be thrown in jail because the local law is crooked. Shenton has a bad habit of turning prisoners loose when it suits him. Say your prayers. You've had your chance to play along but you've overplayed your hand this time and I'm gonna cut my losses.'

'You think you know what's going on around here but you don't know a damned thing.' Nolan spoke quickly in the hope that Lew would hold his fire. 'I could tell you a thing or two that would make your hair curl, and without that knowledge you don't stand a chance of winning this game.'

'You've got ten seconds to convince me you're on the level.' Lew tilted the muzzle of his gun until it pointed between Nolan's eyes. The deadly aperture gaped at Nolan like the gateway to hell.

'The railroad is coming through this county,' Nolan said tensely. 'That's why they're buying up cow spreads. There are fortunes to be made along the right of way. The government will pay thousands of dollars to smart men, and give away shares in the railroad business to those who have been clever enough to buy up the land the railroad needs.'

Lew stared at Nolan while he considered the man's words. Was that what this was all about? Had his father been killed because of some man's greed?

'So who's running the business?' Lew asked.

'You've seen Shenton in action. He's as crooked as a twisted fence post. He's in it for the money. They got rid of Sheriff Parrish, and moved Shenton in to run the law in their favour.'

'I know about Shenton and Mitchell, and I know Jack Tate is involved. But who are the men at the top? They're the ones I want to get at.'

'Abe Fenner at the bank gives Shenton his orders. I don't know details for certain, but look at a map and you'll see that the ranches they've taken over are almost in a straight line north to south. They took Circle H, and got the purchase price back when Tate killed your father. Now they're working on Wishart, because the railroad surveyor wants to run tracks north through Box W and on to Kansas City.'

'You haven't told me anything yet that I don't already know, except that the railroad is interested in those spreads you mentioned,' Lew said. 'Is that all you've got to offer?'

Nolan began to feel uneasy. Lew's expression showed no mercy.

'Shenton told us when he showed up at the Circle H that he killed Faylen in town, and then rode out to Box W and shot Wishart and the other two cowpunchers on the payroll. They're getting ready to take over that spread. They are running behind schedule and need to pull out all the stops.'

'Joe Wishart is dead?' Lew stared aghast at Nolan. 'Did Shenton mention killing anyone else at Box W?'

'He didn't mention anyone else.' Nolan shrugged.

Lew regarded Nolan intently while he considered what he had learned. He needed to get back to Box W. He thrust his gun muzzle under Nolan's nose. Nolan cringed visibly.

'I can't take you with me because you're on foot,' Lew said, 'so I'll turn you loose, and you'd better heed my warning. If I set eyes on you again after this I'll shoot you on sight. Now get out of here, and keep going until you cross the nearest border. Do you get my drift? Get yourself a long way from here.'

'You'll never see me again,' Nolan said fervently. 'I'll wait for Miller to bring me a fresh mount and then skedaddle.'

'Then start walking back to Circle H to meet Miller, and you want to hope that I don't change my mind and come back looking for you.'

Nolan turned instantly and started walking fast towards the distant ranch.

Lew turned the horse and rode on towards Box W. He glanced back from time to time before Nolan was out of sight to check his progress. When Nolan passed from view over a ridge, Lew spurred the horse and rode fast for the Wishart spread. . . .

Jane Wishart had been talking to Wayne Harper in an upstairs room when they heard the shots that killed her father. Jane ran to the window and peered out, but could see nothing. She turned instinctively to run down the stairs, her first thought being that Tulse had somehow got out of the store and found a gun. Wayne grasped her arm, and shook his head when she looked at him to protest.

'That's not a good idea,' he said. 'You stay here and I'll take a look.'

Jane listened to the echoes of the shots and was gripped by a terrible fear. 'My father could be hurt,' she gasped. She went along to her father's bedroom, almost dragging Wayne with her, for he would not let go of her arm, and she pulled her father's pistol from his gun-belt, which was hanging on the inside of the door. She cocked the weapon, shook herself free of Wayne's grasp, and went to the top of the stairs. She paused when she heard Shenton's voice, and when Tulse answered she started down the stairs holding the pistol almost at arm's length before her.

Shenton and Tulse had left the house by the time Jane reached the ground floor. Wayne stayed at her side, and, when they entered the big front living room, Wayne ran across to the fireplace and snatched down the Winchester rifle hanging there. He checked the weapon, found it fully loaded, and jacked a shell into the breech. Jane went to one of the windows and peered out. She could see Shenton and Tulse over by the corral, and when she dropped her gaze to the porch she was struck with horror, for she could see and recognize one of her father's legs.

'Pa's down on the porch, Wayne,' she gasped.

He grabbed her again when she made a move to run to the front door.

'They'll kill you if you show yourself, Jane,' he said.

She shook herself free of his hand and jerked open the

door. Wayne grasped her, permitting her only to stick her head outside to look at the porch. When she saw her father's body slumped on the sun-warped boards and a great amount of his blood spread out around his head, she froze in horror and the pistol dropped from her hand.

'Pa's dead on the porch,' she whispered through stiff lips. 'Shenton killed him.'

'How do you know it was Shenton?' Wayne demanded.

'I heard his voice, and recognized it. He's over by the corral now, with the prisoner from the storeroom.'

'I'll check your pa,' Wayne said.

'No. Wait. They'll ride by in a moment and we can shoot them.'

'You can't just shoot a sheriff without proof,' Wayne protested.

'You would if it was your father who'd been killed,' Jane replied. She picked up the pistol, cocked it, and then moved to a window. Moments later, Shenton and Tulse rode by on their way to the gate. Jane opened a window and fired at them. Shenton spurred his horse, followed by Tulse, and they disappeared along the trail to town.

Jane dropped the pistol and went out to the porch. Wayne followed her, and led her back into the house when he saw that Joe Wishart was indeed dead. . . .

When Lew rode into the yard of Box W the first thing he saw was Joe Wishart sprawled on the porch. He dismounted quickly and stomped towards him, staring in disbelief at the dead rancher. A movement at the window overlooking the porch attracted his gaze and he looked up to see Wayne peering out at him. He hurried to the door and entered the house. Jane was seated on a chair at the table, her chin in a cupped hand, her eyes glazed with shock as she stared blindly into the distance.

'What happened here?' Lew demanded.

'It was the sheriff who shot Joe,' Wayne said. 'Jane saw him in the yard. He freed the prisoner from the store-room, and they both rode off towards town. Why would the sheriff shoot Joe?'

'Because he's bad right through, and working with the badmen,' Lew replied. He looked at Wayne, saw the scar of the wound his brother had received at the hands of Jack Tate, and again wondered how Wayne had survived the shooting. 'I saw him riding in this direction when I left here earlier.' He turned to Jane and spoke to her but she did not answer, sitting motionless as if she hadn't heard his voice. 'Jane,' he said more loudly, and reached out to touch her shoulder. 'Snap out of it, Jane. Tell me what you saw.'

Jane was startled by his touch, and looked around as if awakening from a deep sleep. Her eyes seemed vacant, but Lew saw animation seeping back into her gaze. She heaved a deep sigh, and then began to weep softly.

'I'm sorry, Jane, but I need to know what happened here. Did you see Shenton shoot your father?'

'No,' she said tremulously. 'I heard his voice after the shots. He came into the house and turned your prisoner loose. I recognized Shenton's voice when he spoke to the prisoner as they left the house. They rode out together, heading for town. I shot at them but missed. Why would the sheriff shoot my father, Lew?'

'I'll ask Shenton when I see him,' Lew said grimly.

'Where are your two punchers? They were here when I rode out.

'They're dead,' Wayne said. 'I had a look around and found both of them shot. What's going on, Lew?'

'Too much, and I haven't the time to explain to you now. I want to head for town and get answers to some more questions bothering me.'

'I'll ride with you.' Wayne picked up the rifle he had been carrying.'

'No. You stay here with Jane and watch out for her, although I don't think she'll be bothered now. I don't want either of you getting mixed up in this. Stay put until I come back, OK?'

'Sure, if you say so.' Wayne nodded and went to the window to peer around the yard.

'I'll get back to you as soon as I can.' Lew looked at Jane's impassive face, shook his head, and hurried to the door.

'Don't take any chances,' Wayne called after him.

Lew grimaced and went out to his horse. He swung into the saddle and set off at a fast clip for the distant town. He knew enough about the situation to be able to work out what had been going on, and he had pinpointed some of the culprits, so it was time to start a reckoning, to pay some of the debts that had been accruing. He wanted to discover where his father was buried, and would not stop until every last badman had been confronted and made to pay the ultimate price for his wrongdoing. He pushed on to Bostock with death in his gun and in his heart.

# NINE

Buck Shenton was thoughtful as he rode back to town from Box W with Tulse tagging along behind. Reviewing the day's events, he became aware that his mind was filled with an increasing sense of unease, although, to his way of thinking, nothing had gone wrong. He had stopped Faylen's big mouth, killed Joe Wishart to clear the way for the next phase of the land-grab, and had murdered Buster Nelson out at Circle H to open up the possibility of arresting Lew Harper for the killing. There were no loose ends. But instead of feeling pleased with his activities his senses were swamped with a growing sense of imminent disaster.

Had he made a mistake somewhere that was not obvious? He ran over the sequence of events again and shook his head. Nothing had gone wrong, and, anyway, he was the county sheriff and could arrange incidents how he pleased, so long as they were not witnessed. But he had to admit that he was uneasy, and could not pinpoint the reason why.

He glanced at Tulse, who was aware that he had killed Wishart, and further disquiet filled his mind. When he saw the buildings of Bostock showing in the distance he had reached the conclusion that Tulse was a danger to his future.

'Hey, Tulse, why in hell did you shoot Joe Wishart?' he demanded.

'What, me?' Tulse was shocked. 'What are you talking about? I was locked in that storeroom at the ranch when the shots that killed him were fired.'

Shenton grinned. 'I think you're lying,' he said. 'You even look like the killer.'

Tulse's expression changed and he shook his head. 'You're not going to pin that on me,' he snarled. 'What gives?'

'It's simple. Either you killed the rancher or I did, and as I'm the sheriff of this county it looks like you're gonna have to carry the can.'

It took Tulse a few moments to get the drift of Shenton's words, and when it finally dawned on him he straightened in his saddle.

'You can't get away with that!' he declared.

'Whose word do you think they'll take, huh, yours or mine?' Shenton watched Tulse closely, saw his expression change, and was ready when Tulse reached for the pistol tucked in his waistband. Tulse dragged the gun clear and thumbed back the hammer, but Shenton beat him to the draw, levelled his gun and blasted a shot into Tulse's chest. Tulse died instantly and fell out of his saddle. Blood leaked from his body and soaked into the arid ground.

Shenton dismounted, threw Tulse face-down across the saddle, and continued to town. He rode into the livery barn, leading Tulse's horse, and dismounted. Amos Haine, an odd-job man in town, appeared in the doorway of the little office and came hurrying forward when he saw Shenton.

'I've been waiting for you to get back, Sheriff,' he called. 'Ed Faylen was found in a stall along there this morning, and that killer horse of his was with him. He must have been moving the horse from out back and it kicked him to death.'

'Faylen is dead?' Shenton demanded.

'That's right. I'm gonna be running this place now. Mrs Faylen came after me when Ed was found. This is the first regular job I've had in years.'

'Watch out you don't get drunk and lose it,' Shenton replied. He turned and dragged Tulse's body from the saddle. 'Fetch the undertaker to take care of this stiff,' he added.

'Who is he?' Haine demanded, bending to look into Tulse's face. 'He's a stranger.'

'I don't know him either, but I know what he did. I saw him shoot Joe Wishart out at Box W. Seems he was riding the chuck line, and killed Wishart for no reason at all.'

'Wishart's dead? Jeez! What in hell is going on around here?'

'That ain't all. I rode into Circle H earlier and found Buster Nelson dead. Lew Harper rode in there and shot him, and I'm looking for Harper to charge him with the murder.'

'Nelson was working at Circle H,' Haine mused. 'Casey Mitchell owns the place now. So what was Harper doing out there? His old man used to own the spread.'

'Take care of these horses when you've got Will Benton

in here for this body,' Shenton said. 'I've got a lot to do yet before I can finish for the day.'

Haine ran out of the barn and hurried along the street calling the news of the murders to everyone he met. Shenton followed slowly, looking around as he made his way to the law office. He ignored the curious townsmen, entered the office, and slammed the door. The first thing he did was check his prisoners. Jack Tate was lying on a bunk in one of the three single cells, nursing his chest wound. His fleshy face looked pale, strained, and shock was showing in his dark eyes. Hanks sat in the adjoining cell, resting on the end of his bunk and staring into space.

'Where the hell have you been, Shenton?' Tate demanded. 'I need a drink. You should get a guard in here when you ride out. They treat cattle better than this.'

'If you don't stop complaining the minute I come in I'll toss you out of here on your ear,' Shenton replied. 'You're better off than your pard Tulse – he's dead.'

'Tulse dead?' Tate struggled up from the bunk and came forward to grip the bars of his cell door. 'What happened to him?' he demanded.

'I found him in the yard at Box W. Joe Wishart was dead on his porch, and the two punchers who work there were also dead. That's all I know so don't ask questions.'

'When are you gonna turn me loose?' Hanks demanded. 'I've got things to do.'

'You'll have to wait. I spoke to Fenner before I rode out earlier and he said to keep you in here for a few days. If you don't like it, then take it up with him when I do turn you loose.'

'You sound like things ain't been going right for you,'

Tate observed.

'You can say that again. Lew Harper rode into Circle H and killed Buster Nelson.'

'Turn me loose and I'll go after Harper,' Tate said.

'Not right now.' Shenton shook his head. 'I've got things to do, and hunting Harper ain't one of them.'

He went back into the front office and sat down at his desk. His mood was changing, he realized – not just a momentary thing but an abrupt change in attitude that made this job, and what he was doing, no longer seem attractive. He suddenly wanted to move on. He had an underlying feeling that something had gone or was going wrong, and he did not want to be around to answer any questions when the axe finally fell. He had to get out while the going was good.

He left the office and walked across the street to the bank. Fenner was talking to the teller, and looked up quickly when Shenton called his name.

'Come into my office,' Fenner said quickly, and led the way.

Shenton made a report of his activities during the day, and Fenner's face turned pale as he listened, but he remained silent. When he had listed the murders he had committed, Shenton did not give Fenner a chance to comment.

'And that's that,' he said firmly. 'Now I'm quitting. I want out. I feel it's time to visit new pastures; so pay me what you owe me and I'll split the breeze.'

'Quitting?' Fenner gasped. 'You can't do that at this stage of the business. You knew that when you took the job. And we have an agreement that if you don't see it through to the end you forfeit wages and bonus.'

'Don't try to pull that one on me or you'll be sorry.' Shenton tapped the butt of his holstered gun. 'My reckoning is that you owe me about three thousand dollars, so pay up and I'll kiss goodbye to this burg.'

'It'll take me some time to get that kind of money together. You better let Hanks out of jail and give him your law badge. He'll take over your job. Send him over here to see me.'

'Just don't try to double-cross me,' Shenton warned. 'I'll give you till morning, but that's all. If you don't go along with my wishes then I'll blow this whole scheme of yours wide open. Get that straight, do like I tell you, and you'll have no trouble from me.'

'There'll be no trouble,' Fenner said.

Shenton returned to the law office. He let Hanks out of the cell and followed him into the front office. Hanks kept going, but paused when Shenton called his name.

'Fenner says you're to take over as sheriff.' Shenton removed his star and tossed it to Hanks, who caught it deftly and stood looking at it as if he had never seen a law badge before.

'What are you gonna do?' Hanks demanded suspiciously.

'I've quit, and I'm moving on tomorrow. Pin that badge on your shirt and then go see Fenner. He'll tell you what he wants done.'

'I finished with law work when I left Kansas City,' Hanks protested, 'and came west because I wanted to get away from it all. So I ain't cut out to be a sheriff.'

'That's your problem. Tell Fenner when you see him.

Before you go, what about Tate? Are you going to turn him loose?'

'You do what you think is right,' Hanks replied. 'I'm not taking on the job. If Fenner tries to make me, I'll quit.'

Shenton shrugged. 'It's your business. I'll turn Tate loose now. If you want to put him back behind bars he'll be around town.'

Shenton returned to the cell block and unlocked the door of Tate's cell.

'Get out, Tate, and make yourself scarce. If you want some advice then put a lot of distance between yourself and this place.'

'What's wrong?' Tate demanded. 'Where's your badge?'

'I've quit, and if you've got any sense you'll do the same.'

'I'll talk to Fenner.' Tate left the cell block in a hurry, and was gone from the office by the time Shenton reached the connecting door.

Hanks had already departed. Shenton picked up some personal belongings and walked out of the office. He crossed the street to Ma Logan's guest house, where he was living, and prepared to pull out in the morning.

Hanks went into the bank and found Abe Fenner waiting for him.

'What's this all about, Mr Fenner?' Hanks asked. 'Shenton told me he's quit. Has something gone wrong with your plans?'

'Nothing's wrong. You will carry on as the sheriff in Shenton's place.'

'I don't want that job, Mr Fenner.'

'Don't give me a hard time, Hanks. Just do it until I can

get someone else to take over. All you need to do is watch out for Lew Harper, and, if he shows up, arrest him on suspicion of murder.'

'Who'd he kill?'

'Someone named Buster Nelson, out at Circle H. Shenton told me about it. You'd better have a few words with Shenton before he leaves. He'll fill you in on details.'

'I'll do that, but I don't like it,' Hanks said.

'Shenton plans to pull out in the morning after I've paid him off. He wants three thousand dollars. Follow him when he leaves town, kill him with no witnesses, and you can pocket the money he's carrying as a bonus for the job.'

Hanks smiled. 'On second thoughts I think I might like the job of sheriff,' he said.


Cleaver Nolan was waiting impatiently when Miller returned from Circle H with two fresh horses.

'You took your sweet time,' he rasped. 'Harper doubled back after you left, and got the drop on me. I'm getting out of here fast before he comes back again.'

'I ain't running,' Miller snarled. 'I've got some wages to come from Mitchell. I'll collect them before I think of quitting. Come into town with me and we'll see Mitchell together. It'll be time to quit after we've got what's owing to us.'

Nolan climbed into the saddle of the horse Miller had brought for him. He felt easier with Miller at his side.

'OK,' he said. 'Let's get on to town. But I ain't staying. I'm getting outa here soon as I can.'

They covered the ten miles to Bostock and stopped off at the saloon. Casey Mitchell was in his office, and they walked in on him.

'What are you two doing in town?' Mitchell demanded. 'Who's taking care of the ranch?'

'Harper has been there,' Nolan said, 'and there was hell to pay. I want my wages and then I'm pulling out. I'm all washed up around here.'

'Harper has scared you, huh?' Mitchell sat back in his seat and grinned. 'What about you, Miller?'

'I'm thinking I'll stay on,' Miller said, fishing for promotion. 'I don't run from anyone. But I'll want to be top dog out at Circle H if I stay on.'

'You've got the job.' Mitchell spoke without hesitation. 'Get on back out to the ranch and take over. Nolan, if you're finished on the range you might wanta take on a job as deputy sheriff. Hanks took over from Shenton, but he wants help. The job's yours if you fancy it.'

Nolan shook his head. 'No. I told you I'm quitting, and nothing you can say will make me change my mind. I want out.'

'OK. I'll settle up in the morning. Now get out of here. I'm real busy.'

Lew eased his mount when he sighted Bostock in the distance, and had to fight down the murderous impulses flaring in his mind. He had no clear idea how to handle the situation facing him, and realized that he couldn't go in shooting wildly at the guilty men because they had the law on their side, and if he didn't play it smart he would quickly wind up dead. He rode to the rear of the stable, put his horse into an empty stall, and made his way to the office. He looked in to see the new stableman seated at the desk, and recalled that Nolan had told him that Shenton had killed Faylen.

Lew moved away from the office and left by the rear door. He strode along the back lots, waiting for sundown to cover his movements, and tried to formulate a plan for attacking his enemies. Shadows were already gathering in corners and alleys, and Lew fought against tiredness and hunger. The bullet wound in his left thigh, although just a flesh wound, was throbbing painfully. He reached the far end of town and stood at a corner to look along the street. The town seemed deserted. He walked across the street and moved along the back lots to the rear of Doc Allen's house. When he knocked on the back door it was opened by Mrs Allen. She was surprised to see him.

'I need to see Doc, Mrs Allen,' Lew said, 'and I don't want to be seen in town right now.'

'Doc has been worried about you, Lew,' she replied. 'Come on in.'

He followed her to the doctor's office, and Doc Allen sprang up from his seat when Mrs Allen announced him.

'Lew, where have you been? You've missed all the action around here.'

'I've had enough of my own to handle,' Lew replied. 'There's been murder on the range today. Shenton killed Joe Wishart this afternoon, and he murdered Ed Faylen earlier.'

'Shenton is telling everyone in town that you killed Buster Nelson out at Circle H. He brought in a dead man named Tulse, and said Tulse killed Wishart. Faylen was found trampled to death by his wild stallion. But Shenton has quit as sheriff. He's leaving town tomorrow.'

'He's quit?' Lew sighed as he saw his plan for ending the local trouble tumbling to pieces.

'And that ain't all. Ossie Hanks, Fenner's bank guard, has taken over as sheriff, and he's got a deputy by the name of Miller.'

'I don't believe it!' Lew was shocked by the news.

'And Jack Tate has been turned loose. I saw him in the saloon with Casey Mitchell just a little while ago – celebrating.'

'Hanks shot me last night,' Lew mused. 'Miller and Nelson set a gun trap for me yesterday afternoon. Hanks shot Pete Elrington in the stable. And you say I'm being blamed for all the mayhem that's going on? Apart from that, I learned today that Jack Tate was bragging in prison that he killed my father three years ago. When I talked to Abe Fenner about my pa he showed me a card at the bank which proved that Pa opened an account there with the money he received from the sale of Circle H. How could he have done that if he was murdered by Tate?'

Doc Allen shook his head. 'All of this adds up to one hell of a crooked business,' he observed. 'You've got to put pressure on someone in the know, and crack the business open like a nut, although it looks to be too tough a nut to be cracked. But Shenton has quit so it looks like he's had enough. If you could make him talk you might get the deadwood on all the others involved.'

'I feel I oughta go for Tate first,' Lew said firmly, as if he had already decided on his plan of action. 'He killed my father, and I'd like to see him taken down and done for before I go up against the others, just in case I don't make it. I'm ready to die fighting this thing, but if I go, I want

Jack Tate to go before me. Apart from that, there's one chance I might have of pulling this off. If I took over the sheriff's job around here, just for the clean-up, I might come out on top.'

'It's a long shot,' Doc Allen mused. 'But I've got a better idea. I'll scoot around town and talk to the mayor, William Goldwyn, and some others on the town council, and see if they will appoint you town marshal.'

'OK, see what you can do. I'll move in on Hanks right now and put him out of it.'

'And I'll see you at the law office with word of Goldwyn's decision. You're gonna have to do it alone, you know, Lew.' Doc Allen spoke tensely. 'There's no one in town will step forward to help you. And I don't think you can do it on your own. They'll trample you into the dust before you can get started, and with you gone the badmen will get everything their own way.'

'I'll get started then.' Lew glanced through the office window; he saw that the shadows had lengthened and the sun was on the point of going down beyond the western horizon, and knew it was time to go to work. The outcome was in the balance, but that knowledge did not sway him from his determination to fight to the death to right the wrongs that had been committed against his family. The coming darkness would cloak the action he planned, and it would all be ended, one way or another, before the sun showed in the morning. . . .

141

# TEN

Doc Allen left his home to do what he could on Lew's behalf and Lew departed when the shadows were dense enough to cover his movements. He walked stealthily across the deserted street and gained the cover of the alley mouth beside the jail. When he looked through the big front window into the law office he saw Ossie Hanks seated inside, his feet up on the desk and a bottle of whiskey in front of him. Lew drew his pistol and checked it. He had to make a start somewhere, and at the moment Hanks looked to be the likeliest candidate for attention. Lew did not want the new sheriff to appear at the scene of any action with the power of the law at his back.

The door of the office opened to Lew's touch. He tightened his grip on his gun and stepped across the threshold, closed the door with his left heel, and walked to the desk as Hanks looked up. The big ex-bank guard dropped his feet to the floor and sprang up, but halted when he saw the levelled gun in Lew's right hand.

'What the hell are you doing here?' Hanks demanded.

'What do you suppose?' Lew replied. 'I'll not ask you to come and have a drink with me, that's for sure. I'm gonna put you out of circulation until I've stamped on the men who have been running roughshod around here. So get your hands up, turn around, and I'll take your gun.'

'You're loco,' Hanks blustered. 'I'm the new sheriff here. Shoot me and they'll put a rope around your neck before you know it.'

'What happens to me will not affect you in any way,' Lew replied. 'You'll be dead and out of it. Now turn your back and keep your hands wide.'

'Hold on a minute.' Hanks' big, fleshy face had turned pale. His dark eyes glared like those of a wild animal trapped in a cage. 'You better think about this. There'll be no going back if you disarm me.'

'What do you suggest? That I turn you loose? Last night you followed me out to Box W and tried to kill me. Today you rode into Circle H with orders for Nolan and his crooked crew. Then you killed Pete Elrington. I need you out of it, Hanks.'

'I'll do a deal with you,' Hanks said smoothly. 'I didn't want this job. I ain't mixed up in this business as much as the others, and I'll tell what I know if you let me go afterwards.'

'No dice! Turn around and take what's coming to you.'

'You don't look like a man who'd shoot someone in the back, or commit cold-blooded murder.'

'My father was murdered by Jack Tate, and that's pushed me over the edge. Now do like I tell you or I'll shoot you here and now.'

Hanks half turned away and Lew stepped a half pace to his left, intent on reaching around the big man and relieving him of the gun in his shoulder holster. Hanks moved with surprising speed, clamping his left arm over Lew's left hand as he grasped the hidden gun with his right hand and spun around on his toes. His right fist swung in a short arc and his bunched knuckles came at Lew's head like a battering ram. Lew had no intention of shooting Hanks at that moment, although the new sheriff feared for his life. He lowered his head and pulled in his chin in the split second before Hanks landed his blow.

The big fist crashed against the side of Lew's head just above the left ear, and his senses lurched at the impact. He swung his pistol in an upward motion and hammered the barrel against the back of Hanks' head. The big man's knees weakened at the blow but he threw his left arm around Lew's neck, bearing him to the floor with his massive weight. His right hand struck again in a powerful punch. Lew felt his senses begin to fade. The glare of the lamplight seemed to dim. Desperately, he swung his pistol again and it smashed against Hanks' forehead. Hanks relaxed instantly, his grip slackening, and Lew slid away from him and regained his feet.

Lew staggered as he picked up a bunch of keys from a corner of the desk. He secured a hold on Hanks' collar, exerted his strength to haul the new sheriff into the cell block, and locked him in a cell. Hanks sat up and stared around, then lurched to his feet.

'You won't get away with this,' he yelled as Lew left him.

Lew went back into the front office and sank down on a chair. The wound in his leg was painful but he ignored the discomfort. The street door opened at that moment and Miller came striding into the office, a law star glinting on his chest. Lew palmed his gun, and Miller pulled up as

144

if he had run into a wall. Shock stained his face and he looked around quickly.

'Where's Hanks?' he demanded.

'In a cell; and that's where the rest of your crooked bunch will be before tonight is over,' Lew responded. 'Unbuckle your gun-belt and head for the cells. Your job as a deputy has fallen through.'

Miller seemed dazed by the turn of events, but disarmed himself without hesitation.

'So where's Nolan?' Lew asked as he pushed Miller towards the cell block.

'We parted on the trail where you left him,' Miller lied. 'He took the horse I picked up for him and rode out.'

Lew locked Miller in a cell and went back into the front office. He decided to give Doc Allen a chance and sat at the desk to pass the time. Thirty minutes elapsed in silence, and a sense of mounting tension gripped Lew before footsteps sounded on the boardwalk outside. Lew tensed and put his hand on the butt of his pistol. The street door was opened and Lew heaved a sigh of relief when Doc Allen appeared.

'It went better than I expected,' Doc Allen said, opening his left hand to reveal a silver law star in his palm. Lew saw the words TOWN MARSHAL in the centre of the badge. 'Goldwyn is happy to appoint you. He's been trying to get the town council to do something like this for a long time because he's been unhappy with the way the local law has been operating around here, and he thinks Buck Shenton is no better than a lowdown crook. He jumped at the chance of appointing you when I told him you were a deputy sheriff in Montana. Now it's up to you, Lew, and good luck.'

Lew nodded, and smiled grimly as the doctor came to him and pinned the badge to his shirt front.

'This will come as a shock to some of the townsfolk,' Allen observed, 'but I'll be on hand when there's shooting, just in case my services are needed.'

'I want Shenton next,' Lew said. He opened the bottom drawer of the desk, saw several pairs of handcuffs, and selected a pair. He pushed one cuff under his belt and pulled the short chain halfway through until the cuffs hung suspended over it.

Doc Allen shook his head wordlessly as Lew left the law office. Lew eased his pistol on his hip and strode along the boardwalk. Shenton roomed at Ma Logan's guest house, and Lew did not pause when he reached the front door. He entered and walked into the dining room to find widowed Ma Logan, a short, fleshy, homely-looking woman with grey hair and a motherly face, setting out a long table for the evening meal.

'Howdy, Ma,' Lew greeted.

She looked at him shrewdly. Her eyes fastened on his marshal's star and remained fixed on it. 'Lew Harper,' she said, nodding. 'I heard you'd returned, and not before time. Have you seen your father recently? He hasn't been seen around here for some time.'

'You won't see him around any more,' he replied. 'Is Buck Shenton in?'

'He's up in his room. He told me he's leaving tomorrow.'

'He has a change of plans. He won't be leaving if I have anything to do with it. Where is his room?'

146

'It's the first door on the right at the top of the stairs. But he'll be down in a few minutes.'

'I'll go up and fetch him.' Lew left her and ascended the stairs. He paused outside the first door on the right and listened intently, his ear pressed against the panel, but could hear no sound from inside the room. He drew his pistol and cocked it, then grasped the door handle and turned it slowly. The door opened silently and he lunged inside, swinging his gun to cover the interior of the room, and saw Buck Shenton lying on his back on the single bed. He had been asleep until Lew barged in on him. Now he sat up and made a grab for the butt of his gun, placed close to hand, but Lew's harsh voice stopped his movement.

'Don't try it, Shenton. I need you alive to help me sort out the murders you committed today. Get up and keep your hands where I can see them.'

Shenton gazed at Lew as if mesmerized, and his eyes pulled to mere slits when he saw the marshal's star on Lew's shirt. He got slowly to his feet and held out his wrists as Lew pulled the handcuffs from his belt.

'I should've cleared out earlier, when I had the chance,' Shenton remarked.

Lew jabbed the muzzle of his pistol into Shenton's left side above the waist and locked one of the cuffs around the man's left wrist. Shenton offered no resistance. He held up his right wrist for the other cuff, and Lew snapped it in place.

'Don't give me any trouble,' Lew told him, and pushed him towards the door.

Shenton descended the stairs and Lew followed him

closely, gun in hand. Ma Logan was standing in the doorway of the dining room, her eyes wide in shock. Shenton paused before her.

'I won't be eating here this evening, Ma.' Shenton said.

Lew was distracted for a split second, and at that moment the front door was opened and a man entered. Lew's head jerked around. He saw the newcomer was Cleaver Nolan, and Nolan was already pulling his gun, a curse of astonishment spilling from his lips. Lew stepped to his left but Shenton reacted swiftly and moved in the same direction, shielding Nolan. Lew lifted his pistol and slammed the barrel against Shenton's head. The ex-sheriff sprawled heavily, and Lew was left facing Nolan, who was thumbing back the hammer of his gun. Lew dived to his left as Nolan fired, and the slug plucked at Lew's holster in passing. Lew hit the floor on his left side and raised his gun. He fired when his foresight covered Nolan's chest, and the heavy .45 slug blasted through Nolan's heart.

The racket of the two shots was overpowering in the close confines of the house. Gunsmoke billowed. Lew quickly pushed himself to one knee. Shenton was not moving. Nolan was leaning back against the front door, suspended for a frozen moment, until the life and strength of his body ran out. Then he fell to the floor, his blood dribbling over the carpet. The gun echoes died slowly.

Ma Logan was standing in the background, her mouth open, eyes wide in shock and fright, but she made no sound. Her face was ashen.

'I'm sorry about this, Ma,' Lew said. 'I wanted to do this quietly.'

He bent over Shenton, saw that the ex-sheriff was conscious, and dragged him to his feet, wanting to get him to the jail before the town became aware of what was happening. He dragged Shenton out of the house and hurried him along in the darkness until they reached the law office. Two horses were tethered to the hitch rail outside the jail, and Lew paused and looked around. Then he pushed Shenton forward and they went inside.

Lew blinked in surprise when he saw Jane Wishart seated at the desk and his brother Wayne standing in the doorway leading to the cells. Wayne was holding a double-barrelled shotgun with the butt under his left arm. He turned with a tight smile on his lips.

'What are you two doing here?' Lew demanded.

'We've come to help you,' Wayne replied.

'I warned you to stay out at Box W.'

'You can't finish this on your own,' Wayne protested. 'I'm OK now, and I need to be with you.'

'Now you're here, get the cell keys off the desk and open up a cell for Shenton.'

Wayne grinned and snatched up the bunch of keys. Shenton remained silent as he was locked in a cell. Lew returned to the front office, followed closely by Wayne. Jane had not moved at the desk, and she did not speak, her face proclaiming grief and shock at the death of her father.

'I didn't see Jack Tate in the cells,' Wayne said.

'He's next on my list,' Lew told him. 'You stay here and guard the prisoners. Lock this door when I leave and don't open it to anyone but me. I'll sing out when I come back. Have you got that?'

'Sure.' Wayne nodded.

Lew departed then, his mind concentrating on what he needed to do. He kept to the shadows and headed for the saloon. A dozen men were inside, some drinking at the bar and others gambling at small tables. There was no sign of Casey Mitchell, and the bartender was a stranger to Lew – big, fleshy, and looking well able to take care of himself in any situation. There was no sign of Jack Tate, and Lew considered his next move.

He decided to pick up Abe Fenner, and made his way along the street to a turn-off into a quieter street where the business folk of the town lived in decent houses. There was a light in the front window of Fenner's house. Lew drew a deep breath, restrained it for a moment, and then exhaled slowly to rid himself of tension. He dropped his hand to the butt of his gun and rapped on the door with his left hand. Moments passed, and just when he thought there would be no answer the door was opened silently. Abe Fenner appeared – lamplight streaming out through the doorway.

'Lew, what do you want at this time of the day?' Fenner demanded.

'Something that won't wait,' Lew replied.

'Then you'd better come in.' Fenner stepped aside and Lew crossed the threshold. 'What's so important it can't wait until the morning?'

Lew closed the front door with his left heel and placed his back against it. Fenner's expression hardened as he caught Lew's mood, and then he saw the law star on Lew's chest.

'Why are you wearing a marshal's badge?' Fenner demanded.

'It gives me the power to arrest lawbreakers.' Lew smiled tensely. 'You've broken just about every law in the book these past few years, but I've got the deadwood on you. I've arrested Hanks, your new sheriff, and Miller, who was acting as his deputy, and, just to keep the record straight, I've put Buck Shenton behind bars. Now it's your turn, Fenner. I'm arresting you on suspicion of being involved in murder, fraud, and land-grabbing.'

'This is preposterous!' Fenner's face had paled, and his lips barely moved as he protested. 'Who has made these allegations against me?'

'Rats start squealing when they're cornered,' Lew replied. 'I've learned a lot about your crooked business – buying ranchers out, stealing the sale price back from them, and, in my father's case, having him murdered. I know you've done that, and all because the railroad is coming through this county. Need I say more?'

Lew paused, but Fenner made no response; too badly shocked to speak.

'Shenton is in jail for murdering Joe Wishart out at Box W this afternoon, and he killed a man named Tulse, who broke out of prison with Jack Tate. I haven't got Tate yet, but he's on my list. So let's put you behind bars and then I'll pick up Casey Mitchell, one of your partners in this crooked business.'

'I want to see Walt Carson, the lawyer,' Fenner said thickly.

'All in good time!' Lew opened the front door. 'Let's do this quietly. You know where the jail is, so head for it.'

Fenner stumbled through the shadows like a man living in a bad dream. Lew grasped the banker by an arm and held him tightly. He called out when they reached the law office, and Wayne, holding a shotgun ready for action, opened the door suspiciously, grinning when he saw Fenner.

'I need to keep Fenner away from the other prisoners until I've collected statements from each of them,' Lew mused. 'There are a couple of spare cells upstairs, so we'll put him up there. Bring the keys, Wayne. And I'd better see if a couple of townsmen will come in here as special deputies to keep an eye on these prisoners.'

Fenner was locked in an upper cell. Lew prepared to venture out again. He paused by the street door.

'I'm going after Casey Mitchell now,' he told Wayne.

'I'd like to go with you,' Wayne said.

'You're doing a good job here,' Lew replied. 'I'd be stuck in here without your help.'

Wayne nodded, but he was not happy. Lew took his leave and returned to the saloon. His eyes glittered when he peered over the batwings and saw Casey Mitchell emerge from behind the bar and head towards his office at the rear of the big public room. There was still no sign of Jack Tate in the saloon, though Lew had expected the killer to be around. He looked over the men present, and decided that at least two of them were hardcases working for Mitchell. He decided to try the rear entrance to avoid tangling with any opposition.

The alley at the side of the saloon was in darkness, and Lew loosened his Colt in its holster as he felt his way to the back lots. His eyes became accustomed to the shadows and he paused at the back door of the saloon to try his luck. He uttered a silent prayer when the door opened to his touch. He drew his gun and cocked it as he entered.

He was in a short passage, a door at the end which led into the bar. The door to a storeroom was on the right; the office door to the left. A crack beneath the office door permitted a bar of light to show in the passage, and Lew went to the door, opened it and entered quickly, surprising Mitchell, who was seated at his desk. The office was sparingly furnished. There was just a desk, a metal filing cabinet and a small but sturdy safe standing in a corner.

Mitchell looked up. His right hand moved towards the right-hand drawer in the desk when he recognized Lew, but he paused when Lew made a threatening gesture with his pistol.

'What do you want?' Mitchell demanded. 'I'm busy.'

'I've come to arrest you.' Lew liked the way Mitchell's expression changed.

'Are you loco? Why would you want to arrest me?'

'I guess you know that better than me. You're about the last man I need to arrest, apart from Jack Tate. Your land-grabbing business is over, Mitchell. I've got Fenner behind bars, along with Shenton, Hanks and Miller. So don't act innocent. Get up and come with me.'

Shock stained Mitchell's face. His mouth sagged open but he could say nothing. When Lew motioned with his gun, Mitchell staggered to his feet. He paused for a moment, his hands resting on the desktop, his head bent forward. Then he straightened and came out from behind the desk. He went to the safe, slammed its door and locked it. He looked around the office before turning to face Lew.

'You won't be able to make anything stick,' he said. 'All

I ever did was to buy your father's ranch. I know nothing about land-grabbing or anything else.'

'You'll get a fair trial,' Lew told him. 'Where have you hidden Jack Tate?'

'Is that what this is about? You're after Tate for shooting your brother, huh?'

'I want him for killing my father,' Lew said harshly.

'So you know about that.'

'What do you know about it?' Lew demanded aggressively.

'Only what Tate told me.'

'Did he tell you where he buried my father?'

'I'll tell you where you can find Tate, and then you can ask him yourself, but you'll have to turn me loose first.'

'No deal,' Lew said firmly.

'You wanta give your father a good Christian burial, don't you? He's been lying in an unmarked grave for three years.'

'If you know what's good for you then you'll tell me what you know.' Lew lifted his pistol. 'I'm in no mood for pussy-footing around.'

Mitchell gazed at Lew for some moments, evidently considering the situation. Lew waited. He was in no hurry.

'I'll tell you where Tate is if you'll leave me free for tonight. Come tomorrow, I'll be gone; you won't ever see me again and you'll have Tate in your hands.'

'I wouldn't trust you as far as I could throw a wagonload of fence posts,' Lew replied. 'I'm not worried about Tate. I'll catch up with him in due course. Now let's get moving. I'm putting you behind bars right now. Nobody walks away from this business.'

Mitchell shrugged and walked to the door. Lew closed in on him, and jabbed his gun against his spine.

'It's dark outside,' Lew said. 'Don't try anything or you'll wind up dead.'

Mitchell made no reply and they left the saloon. They reached the law office without incident and Lew yelled to warn Wayne of his presence. The door swung open. Lew pushed Mitchell forward, and, as the saloon man stepped over the threshold, Jane Wishart screamed long and loud.

Guns blasted inside the office. Mitchell stiffened, jerked, and pitched to the floor. Lew heard slugs thudding into the half-open door at his side. He dropped to one knee and lifted his gun as the door swung wide. He saw Shenton standing at the rear of the office, with Miller and Hanks beside him. All were armed, and gunsmoke was swirling across the office. Lew fought down his shock and triggered his pistol. The office rocked to the crash and shock of thunderous gunfire.

Lew's first shot struck Shenton in the chest and the ex-sheriff fell sideways against Hanks, who paused to thrust him aside. Lew saw Miller's gun flame and felt the shock of a slug striking his left arm above the elbow. He sagged against the door post and swung his gun to cover Miller, who fired again, and Lew's pistol roared at the same instant. Miller's slug snarled in Lew's right ear; Lew's slug hit Miller in the stomach. Gunsmoke thickened and Hanks came lumbering forward, his gun uplifted for a shot. Miller fell in front of Hanks, who stumbled over him. Hanks fell to his hands and knees, losing his gun in the process, and, as he scrabbled on the floor for the weapon, Lew lunged forward and slammed his pistol against the new sheriff's head. Hanks subsided, and Lew kicked the discarded pistol into a corner.

Gun echoes seemed to cling to the confines of the office, as if reluctant to fade. Lew blinked rapidly, his eyes smarting from the pungent powder smoke. His left arm felt as if it were broken, and it hung uselessly at his side. He looked around quickly. Shenton was motionless, face-down, as was Miller, and both were bleeding copiously. He checked the inert form of Casey Mitchell, who was dead, killed by his crooked partners in crime. Jane Wishart was seated behind the desk, frozen in horror, eyes staring and face ashen. Her mouth was open but she was silent now, shocked rigid.

Lew looked for his brother, but there was sign of him. He bent over Hanks, dragged him upright, shook him, and stuck the muzzle of his pistol under the big man's nose.

'Where's my brother,' he rapped.

Hanks shook his head and sagged against a wall. 'Hold it. Don't shoot me. Your brother is in the cells,' he gasped. 'He's alive. Shenton didn't shoot him because it would have alerted you. It gave us the chance to set a trap for you, and it would have worked if that girl hadn't screamed.'

'How did you get out of the cells?' Lew demanded.

Hanks forced a bitter laugh. 'Shenton was full of tricks. He always feared he would be exposed for what he was, and hid cell keys in the three cells in case he was ever locked in. He called your brother in and jumped him.'

'On your feet and get back in your cell,' Lew snapped.

With Hanks safely under lock and key once more, Lew

turned his attention to Wayne, who was locked in an adjacent cell. His brother was standing at the cell door, gripping the bars with both hands. He relaxed visibly at the sight of Lew unharmed.

'I'm sorry, Lew,' Wayne said. 'I've let you down.'

'Don't worry about it,' Lew unlocked the cell door. He led the way back into the office. 'Fetch Doc Allen, will you?'

'Sure.' Wayne hurried off, pleased to be able to do something constructive.

Lew went to Jane's side. 'How are you?' he asked.

She shook her head and did not speak.

Lew patted her shoulder, knowing how she must be feeling. He sat down on a corner of the desk and reloaded the empty chambers of his pistol while waiting for Wayne to return with Doc Allen. His thoughts were bitter. The man he really wanted to arrest was Jack Tate, and Tate was the only one who had so far eluded him.

Wayne came back with Doc Allen, who checked the men lying on the floor, found them all dead, and then set about treating Lew's arm.

'I didn't think you'd get this far,' Doc Allen commented. 'Thank God it's over.'

'It isn't,' Lew replied. 'I haven't got Tate yet, and I can't find him in town.'

'I'll help you look for him,' Wayne said eagerly.

'I'm wearing the law badge,' Lew replied. 'You'll be better off in here, guarding the prisoners.'

'But this is different,' Wayne said earnestly. 'Tate shot me and killed Pa. I want to be in at his death.'

'I don't reckon to kill him,' Lew said patiently. 'I want

him to stand trial and then hang for what he did.'

Wayne turned away and picked up a pistol. Lew stared at him for a moment and then turned away. The street door opened and Ben Tropman, the town carpenter, looked into the office.

'Hey, I thought you oughta know,' Tropman said. 'I heard that Jack Tate busted out of prison. I just saw him sneaking into the livery barn. He's probably gonna steal a horse.'

'Thanks.' Lew hitched up his gun-belt and ran from the office.

He went along the street, turned into an alley, and reached the back lots. When his eyes became accustomed to the darkness, he headed for the stable, and sneaked through the big rear door. He stood in deep shadow, watching and listening, but all he heard was the occasional stamp of a hoof and the shuffling and snorting of horses. A dim lamp was burning over the front door on the street, but the rest of the barn was in near-darkness.

Lew moved around silently, peering into darkened stalls, looking for Tate. He paused at the foot of the ladder leading up to the loft and listened intently, hearing nothing suspicious. The lamp suspended in the front doorway cast a dim yellow glow that formed nothing more than a patch of deceptive, unreal shadow. Lew kept his right hand on the butt of his holstered gun and tried to pierce the surrounding shadows.

He heard a sudden rustling sound, and his nerves jumped. He looked around, trying to pinpoint the source of the unnatural noise, and at that moment a large bale of sweet-smelling hay dropped on him from the loft. He was knocked to the ground, and lay for a moment, dazed by the impact. When he heard feet pounding down the nearby ladder he was galvanized into action; he thrust the bale aside, and sprang to his feet. When he reached for his gun he discovered that his holster was empty. Then a pistol barrel crashed against his skull and he plunged forward into a black pit, which seemed to open up at his feet.

Desperation dragged Lew back from the precipice of unconsciousness and he got to his hands and knees. The muzzle of a pistol was pressed against the nape of his neck and he froze.

'It's my lucky day, Harper,' said Jack Tate. 'I've been looking for you and here you are. Say your prayers before I squeeze the trigger. You're a dead man.'

Lew shook his head to try and clear his senses. He looked up to see the dim figure of Tate standing over him, lamplight glowing ghastly on his sweating face.

'Where did you bury my father after you killed him?' Lew demanded.

'You should be wondering where I'm gonna bury you,' Tate chuckled. 'But you're in your last minute alive, so I'll tell you where I put your old man. I caught him sneaking around Circle H after we'd run him out. I shot him in the back, dumped him in a ditch back of the corral there, and kicked the earth over him. Now get up and take it in the chest. I got your brother, and now it's your turn.'

Lew pushed himself upright and tensed to lunge at Tate, aware that he had no alternative but to resist. But Wayne spoke from the shadows behind Tate.

'You didn't do a good job on me, Tate,' Wayne said. 'I'm still breathing. So you killed our pa, huh? Let's see how good you are at dying.'

Tate whirled around, moving surprisingly fast, his pistol lifting to cover Wayne. A gun flashed in the shadows, and, as the shot crashed out, Tate was swept off his feet and fell on top of Lew, who thrust him off and grabbed for his gun. Wayne stepped forward out of the shadows, a pistol steady in his right hand.

'I'm sorry I disobeyed your orders, Lew,' he said.

Lew staggered to his feet. His ears were throbbing from the noise of the shot and he felt all in. His leg was hurting like hell, but his mind was clearing of the cloud that had descended on him from the moment he had reached home range. He knew there were still many questions to be answered, and guilt had to be apportioned, but the men involved, the prime movers, were behind bars, and their turn would come. He put an arm around Wayne's shoulders and they left the barn, leaving Jack Tate lying dead and gun echoes fading away to silence.

'What happens now?' Lew asked as they walked to the law office. 'I've just realized that we have no home and no jobs.'

'Jane's gonna need us,' Wayne observed. 'She'll be all alone on Box W. I reckon she'll welcome us with open arms.'

'When she gets over the shock of her pa's death,' Lew said, 'I want to get Circle H back. I guess time will take care of everything.'

'It'll take care of all of us,' Wayne replied sagely.